THE CAPTIVE TEMPLE

The epic begins . . .

STAR WARS®

E P I S O D E I

THE PHANTOM MENACE™

By Patricia C. Wrede

Based on the screenplay and story by George Lucas

See Episode I through their eyes . . .

STAR WARS®

E P I S O D E I

JOURNAL

Anakin Skywalker

Queen Amidala

Darth Maul

. . . and more to come

Before there was *The Phantom Menace*, there was . . .

STAR WARS®

JEDI APPRENTICE

#1 The Rising Force

#2 The Dark Rival

#3 The Hidden Past

#4 The Mark of the Crown

#5 The Defenders of the Dead

#6 The Uncertain Path

#7 The Captive Temple

. . . and more to come

STAR WARS

JEDI APPRENTICE

The Captive Temple

Jude Watson

LUCAS BOOKS

SCHOLASTIC INC.

New York Toronto London Auckland Sydney
Mexico City New Delhi Hong Kong

No part of this publication may be reproduced in whole or in part, or stored in a retrieval system or transmitted in any form or by any means, electronic, mechanical, photocopying, recording, or otherwise, without written permission of the publisher. For information regarding permission, write to Scholastic Inc., Attention: Permissions Department, 555 Broadway, New York, NY 10012.

ISBN 0-590-51970-0

12 11 10 9 8 7 6 5 4 3 2 1   0 1 2 3 4 5 6/0

Printed in the U.S.A.
First Scholastic printing, April 2000

THE CAPTIVE TEMPLE

The change at the Jedi Temple hit Obi-Wan Kenobi even before he'd stepped inside. The Temple was usually a place of meditation and study, the hushed quiet often interrupted by the sound of soft laughter from behind a closed door, the excited voices of young children, or the faint sound of splashing fountains.

But now the peace is gone, Obi-Wan thought. The quiet felt ominous. It wasn't the quiet of busy souls going about their day. It was the wary hush of a sanctuary under siege.

Obi-Wan stood with his former Master, Qui-Gon Jinn, outside the closed door of the Jedi Council room. At any moment they would be summoned inside. They had been called back to the Temple for the most devastating of reasons — an attack on Jedi Master Yoda's life.

Obi-Wan glanced at Qui-Gon. To an observer, Qui-Gon would seem to possess his usual composure. But Obi-Wan knew better. He could sense the sharp distress that ticked underneath the control.

The Temple was on high security. As always it was completely closed to outsiders. But now even Jedi Knights had been ordered to stay away until further notice. All arrivals and departures were monitored, and no one was allowed to leave except on the most pressing of missions. Even though most of the Jedi knew Qui-Gon by sight, both he and Obi-Wan had to undergo a retinal scan before entering the Temple from the spaceport level.

Qui-Gon's finger tapped the hilt of his lightsaber, then stopped. His face smoothed out, and Obi-Wan knew that Qui-Gon was reaching out to the Force to find his center of calm.

Obi-Wan tried to control his own apprehension. He was burning with questions and speculations, but he did not dare break the silence. Relations between him and his former Master had been strained since Obi-Wan decided he couldn't be Qui-Gon's Padawan any longer. He had renounced his Jedi training in order to help the young people of Melida/Daan bring peace to their planet. Obi-Wan realized now what a mistake he had made. He was a Jedi to the bone. All he wanted was to be accepted back into the order and be Qui-Gon's Padawan again.

Qui-Gon had told Obi-Wan that he'd forgiven him for leaving the Jedi. But if Qui-Gon had truly forgiven him in his heart, why was there this awkward silence between them? Qui-Gon was a reserved man, but Obi-Wan had come to count on the respect and warmth he often saw in his former Master's eyes, as well as his occasional flashes of humor.

Obi-Wan knew that once he was called inside the Council chamber, his own fate might be decided. His heart rose at the thought that perhaps the Council had already voted to accept him back. He had told Yoda that he deeply regretted his decision. He hoped that Yoda might have pleaded his case.

Obi-Wan pressed a hand to his forehead. His increasing anxiety had caused him to perspire. Or was the Temple warmer than normal?

He was about to ask Qui-Gon when the door to the Council room hissed open. Obi-Wan stepped into the room behind Qui-Gon. The twelve Council members ringed the chamber in a semicircle. Gray light flooded the room from the large windows overlooking the white towers and spires of Coruscant. Outside, the wispy clouds looked like thin metallic sheets. An occasional flash of silver shimmered, the wings of a spacecraft catching a ray of sunshine as the clouds momentarily parted.

Obi-Wan had only been in the Council room a few times. He was always awed by the depth of the Force here. With so many Jedi Masters in one space, the air seemed charged.

Immediately his eyes sought Yoda. He was relieved to see the Jedi Master sitting in his usual place, appearing calm and healthy. Yoda's gaze passed over him neutrally, then focused on Qui-Gon. Obi-Wan felt a twinge of worry. He wished Yoda's glance had been more reassuring.

Qui-Gon took his place in the center of the room, and Obi-Wan joined him.

A senior member of the Council, Mace Windu, did not waste time on preliminaries. "We thank you for coming," he said in his dignified way. His eyebrows knit together worriedly. "To be frank, this event has shaken us. Master Yoda rose before dawn to meditate, as is his custom. He went to the Room of a Thousand Fountains, again as is his custom. Before reaching a footbridge he sensed a surge in the dark side of the Force. He hesitated, listening to the Force, and in that heartbeat a device planted underneath the footbridge exploded. The intention was to kill Yoda. Luckily he is not so easily fooled."

Mace Windu paused. A collective shudder seemed to run through everyone in the Council room. So many depended on Yoda's wisdom.

"Mace Windu, here with you now am I," Yoda said gently. "Dwell on the *could haves*, we must not. Focus on the solution, we must."

Mace Windu nodded. "Master Yoda saw the flicker of a meditation robe as someone hurried away. This person ducked underneath a waterfall, then disappeared in the churning surf."

"Strong in the dark side, he was," Yoda said, nodding.

"We know that Bruck Chun hasn't left the Temple since you discovered he was the culprit in the thefts," Mace Windu said to Qui-Gon. "We still do not know who he has allied himself with. We only know there is an intruder in the Temple."

"Has the person been spotted again?" Qui-Gon asked.

"No," Mace Windu said. He reached for a data sheet on the arm of his chair. "But just this morning, a student found this. It was left outside a meditation chamber."

Qui-Gon took the data sheet from Mace Windu's outstretched hand. He read it, then handed it to Obi-Wan.

MEDITATE ON THIS, MASTERS:
NEXT TIME I WILL NOT FAIL.

Mace Windu placed his hands on each arm-rest. "Naturally, this has been the focus of consideration and debate. We feel the dark side working. Not only that, but it appears the invader has managed to sabotage our central power structure. You may have noticed the warmer air. We have a perplexing problem with the air cooling unit. Every time Miro Daroon fixes something in the tech center, there is another malfunction elsewhere. There have also been various problems with the lighting and communication systems in some of the wings of the Temple. Miro is hard-pressed to keep up."

Obi-Wan was puzzled. Mace Windu had not looked at him once during his briefing. Why was he here? He wasn't technically a Jedi, since the Council had not extended the offer to take him back. And he certainly wasn't Qui-Gon's Padawan any longer.

At that moment, every face on the Jedi Council turned to him. Mace Windu's intense gaze studied his face. Obi-Wan struggled to remember his Jedi training in composure. It wasn't easy to have twelve Jedi Masters staring at him. And the penetrating gaze of Mace Windu was the most rigorous of all. His dark eyes had a way of making you feel he had seen into the very heart of you, ferreting out secret feelings you weren't even aware you had.

"Obi-Wan, we are hoping that you will have

insights into what Bruck Chun can and will do," Mace Windu said heavily.

"I wasn't his friend," Obi-Wan said, surprised.

"You were his rival," Mace Windu said. "That could be even more valuable to us."

Obi-Wan was at a loss. "But I didn't know Bruck well. I knew how he would move in a lightsaber duel, yes. But not what was in his mind or heart."

No one said anything. Obi-Wan struggled not to betray his apprehension. He had disappointed the Jedi Masters once more. Looking around the room, he did not meet one friendly eye. Even Yoda gave him no encouragement. He wanted to wipe his damp palms on his tunic, but he didn't dare.

"Of course I'll do whatever I can to help," he added quickly. "Just tell me what you want me to do. I can talk to his friends —"

"No need," Mace Windu interrupted. He laced his long fingers together. "Until a decision is made by the Council, we must ask you not to interfere with Temple business unless we ask you otherwise."

Obi-Wan felt stung. "The Temple is my home!" he cried.

"You are welcome to remain here until your situation is resolved, of course," Mace Windu said. "There is still much discussion to take place."

"But there is a real threat to the Temple," Obi-Wan argued. "You need help. And I wasn't here during the petty thefts. I'm one of the few Jedi students who can be ruled out as a suspect. Someone could have helped Bruck. I could investigate."

Obi-Wan saw with a sinking feeling that he had made a mistake. He should have known better than to ask the Council to take him back based on the fact that he could be of use to them in a crisis.

Mace Windu's sharp gaze cut him like ice. "I think the Jedi can manage to solve the crisis without that kind of help from you."

"Of course," Obi-Wan said. "But I wish to tell all the Jedi Masters that I feel genuine remorse for my decision. It felt right at the time, but I've come to see how wrong it was. I want nothing more than to have back what I once had. I want to be a Padawan. I want to be a Jedi."

"Have again what you had, you cannot," Yoda said. "Different you are. Different is Qui-Gon. Every moment makes you so. Every decision a cost it has."

Ki-Adi-Mundi spoke up. "Obi-Wan, you have violated not only the trust of Qui-Gon, but the trust of the Council. You seem not to recognize this."

"But I do!" Obi-Wan exclaimed. "I take responsibility for it and I'm sorry for it."

"You are thirteen years old, Obi-Wan. You are not a child," Mace Windu said with a frown. "Why do you speak as one? Sorry does not make the offense disappear. You interfered in the internal affairs of a planet without official Jedi approval. You defied the order of your Master. A Master depends on the loyalty of the Padawan, just as the Padawan depends on the Master. If that trust is broken, the bond shatters."

The sting of Mace's words made Obi-Wan wince. He did not expect the Council to be so severe. He couldn't look at Qui-Gon. His gaze found Yoda's.

"Unclear your path is, Obi-Wan," Yoda said with more gentleness. "Hard it is to wait. But wait you must to see your way revealed."

"You may go, Obi-Wan," Mace Windu said. "We must speak with Qui-Gon privately. You may go to your old quarters."

Well, at least that's something, Obi-Wan thought. He struggled to maintain his dignity as he bowed to the Council. But he knew his cheeks burned with shame as he left the room.

CHAPTER 2

Obi-Wan felt relieved as the door hissed behind him. He couldn't face the Masters for one more second. Never in his expectations had he thought his first meeting would go so badly.

He saw a slight figure at the end of the hall, and some of his anxiety lifted. "Bant!" he called.

"I was waiting for you." Bant came toward him, her silver eyes alight. Her salmon skin glowed against a soft blue tunic.

"It's good to see a friend," Obi-Wan admitted.

Bant peered at him. "It did not go well."

"It could not have gone worse."

She slipped her arms around Obi-Wan and hugged him. Obi-Wan caught the scent of salt and sea, a unique scent he always associated with Bant, for on Bant, even salt smelled sweet. As a Calamarian, she was amphibious, needing moisture to live. Her room was kept filled with steam, and she took several swims a day.

"Let's go," Bant murmured.

He didn't have to ask where. They took the lift tube down to the lake level. It was their special spot. After long days of classes and training, there was nothing Bant liked better than to immerse herself in the water for a long swim. Obi-Wan often joined her, or sometimes sat on the bank, watching her gracefully glide underneath the green water.

They exited the lift tube and walked out to what seemed to be a beautiful sunny day on the surface of the planet. But they both knew that the golden sun set in a blue sky was actually a series of illumination banks set high in the domed ceiling. The ground under their feet had been planted with flowering shrubs and leafy trees. Today the lake area was deserted. Obi-Wan could not see anyone swimming, or walking along the many trails.

"Students have been asked to stay in their quarters or the dining halls and meditation rooms if they are not in their classes," Bant said. "It is not an order, merely a request. The attack on Yoda has made us all cautious."

"It was a shocking thing," Obi-Wan said.

"But what about you?" Bant asked. "What did the Council say?"

Bitterness rose in Obi-Wan. "They will not take me back."

Bant looked startled. "They said this?"

Obi-Wan stared out at the lake, his eyes burning. "Well, no, not in those words. But their attitude was very severe. I must wait, they say. Bant, what am I going to do?"

She gazed at him, her large silver eyes full of compassion. "Wait."

He turned away impatiently. "You sound like Yoda."

She put a hand on his arm. "But Obi-Wan, what you did was a serious offense. Not serious enough to get kicked out forever," she added quickly when she saw the look in his eyes. "But the Council will need to see proof of your sincerity. They will need to meet with you several times. They are compassionate, Obi-Wan, but they have the whole Jedi order to protect. It is good that this is so. The Jedi path can be a hard one, and the Council must be sure that your commitment is absolute. That the commitment of *each* of us is absolute."

"My commitment *is* absolute," Obi-Wan said fiercely.

"How can the Council be sure of this, and how can Qui-Gon be sure?" Bant asked with great gentleness. "For you have said that before, when you first joined him."

Anger filled Obi-Wan, an anger fueled by

frustration. He knew that Bant did not want to hurt him. She gazed at him now with concerned, loving eyes, afraid she had offended him.

"I see," he said shortly. "You blame me, too."

"No," she said quietly. "I am telling you that it will take more time than you wish it to take, maybe more time than you think you will be able to bear. But the Council will relent and see what I see."

"And what is that?" Obi-Wan asked, scowling. "An angry boy? A fool?"

"A Jedi," she said softly, and it was the best thing she could have said.

Suddenly, Obi-Wan was struck by a thought. What if the Council took him back, but Qui-Gon did not? If the Council allowed him to remain a Jedi student, he was already thirteen and past the limit to be chosen by a Jedi Knight as a Padawan. Who would ask him, if not Qui-Gon?

He didn't want another Master, Obi-Wan thought in despair. He wanted Qui-Gon.

They had walked to the far side of the lake without Obi-Wan noticing. Here there was a small cove where Bant loved to wade. She stepped into the water, smiling as the coolness washed over her ankles.

"Tell me about Melida/Daan," she said. "No

one knows what happened there. What was it that made you commit to their cause and leave us?"

Obi-Wan froze. Perhaps it was the trace of the smile on Bant's face as she asked the question. Perhaps it was the way the light hit the water, or the way her silver eyes gazed at him trustingly. Perhaps it was the amount of life in that small moment, so beautiful that it blinded him.

He could not tell her about Cerasi. With so much life around him, how could he speak of death?

Obi-Wan was suddenly at a loss for words. He had never had trouble talking to Bant before. But what could he say?

On Melida/Daan, I saw a friend die in front of me. I saw the life in her eyes flicker and dim. I held her in my arms. I felt another beloved friend turn his back on me. A comrade in arms betrayed me. And I betrayed my Master. A string of betrayals and a death that has marked my heart forever.

He could not say any of those things. They lay too deeply in his heart.

When this is over, I'll tell her. When we have time.

"But I want to hear about you," he said, changing the subject. "You look different. Have you grown since I saw you?"

"Maybe a little," Bant said, pleased. Her short height had always bothered her. "And I'm eleven now."

"Soon you'll be a Padawan," Obi-Wan teased.

Bant did not catch his teasing tone. Her eyes were serious as she nodded. "Yes. Yoda and the Council think I am ready."

Obi-Wan was startled. Because of her small size and trusting nature, Bant had always seemed even younger than she was. She had always tagged after him and his best friends Reeft and Garen Muln. "You're young to be chosen," he said.

"It is not age but ability that marks a turning point," Bant answered.

"Now you sound like Yoda again."

Bant giggled. "I am quoting Yoda."

"And what about Garen?" Obi-Wan asked.

"Garen is taking an extra tutorial in piloting," Bant answered. "Yoda thinks his reflexes are especially acute. The Jedi need pilots for missions. He's taking his lesson now in the simulator, or he would have come to see you."

"And where's Reeft?" Obi-Wan asked with a smile. "The dining hall?"

Bant laughed. Their Dresselian friend was known for greedy enjoyment of food. "He was chosen as the Padawan of Binn Ibes. He's off on his first mission."

A pang shot through Obi-Wan. So Reeft was a Padawan now. Bant would be soon. Garen had been chosen for special missions. All of his friends were moving forward as he stood still. No, worse than that. As he moved backward. He had been the first to leave the Temple. Now he would be standing on the landing platform, waving to his friends as they departed, one after the other. He turned away so that Bant couldn't see the longing on his face.

"What about Qui-Gon?" Bant asked. "Do you know if he'll take you back once the Council does?"

Leave it to Bant. She always managed to get to the truth of the issue. Since she spoke what was in her heart, she expected others to do the same.

"I don't know," Obi-Wan said. He bent down to trail a hand in the water, trying to hide his face.

"You know, I thought he was forbidding at first," Bant remarked. "I was a little afraid of him. But I came to see how gentle he is. I'm sure the way will be smoothed between you."

"I didn't know you knew Qui-Gon at all," Obi-Wan said, surprised.

"Oh, yes," Bant said. "I helped him and Tahl with the theft investigation when you were on Melida/Daan."

Curious now, Obi-Wan turned to ask her what she had done, but a strange noise interrupted him. Bant and Obi-Wan looked overhead. A grinding noise filled the air.

They stared up. At first they saw only what they were meant to see: a brilliant sun in a blue sky. Then everything seemed to happen at once. There was a dimming in the light, and suddenly, an object crashed down through the sky, which they could now see was only a scrim. The skeletal forms of catwalks and the blocks of illumination banks were revealed. Part of a horizontal tunnel swung in midair.

"It's the horizontal turbolift," Bant said, horrified. "It's going to crash!"

CHAPTER 3

Obi-Wan saw everything in a flash, but with the clarity of slow motion. The turbolift ran horizontally high above, crossing above the lake and surrounding trails. Normally, it was hidden from view by the glare from the giant illumination banks. But a portion of the lift had fallen through its shaft, knocking out a bank of lights.

"The repulsorlift engines must have blown," Obi-Wan guessed. "It's hanging by a thread."

"That turbolift links the nursery and care centers for the younger children to the dining halls," Bant said, her eyes on it. "It could be filled with children." She wrenched her eyes away.

"I don't have my comlink," Obi-Wan said quickly. "It was damaged on Melida/Daan."

"I'll go," Bant decided. "You stay in case . . . in case it falls."

Bant streaked away. Obi-Wan knew she was heading for the comm unit at the entrance to the lake level. He could not tear his eyes from the turbolift. The shaft swayed slightly. Any moment it could plunge into the lake below.

But the turbolift held.

He couldn't stand around and do nothing. Obi-Wan scanned the tech area overhead. He hadn't realized what a maze of catwalks it was. If the children could climb out of the turbolift, they could escape over the catwalks to the tech service level. . . .

The thought flashed across his mind and he sprinted toward the tech door hidden in the foliage. He burst through and pressed the button for the vertical lift tube. Nothing happened. Obi-Wan turned and saw a narrow staircase heading up.

He took the stairs two at a time, his legs pumping, his muscles tiring as the long climb went on. Still he did not falter.

At last he burst out onto the top level. A tunnel led to a series of doors marked with numbers: B27, B28, B29, and on and on. Which door would lead to a catwalk closest to the damaged turbolift?

Obi-Wan paused. His heart was beating furiously. He wanted to charge ahead, but he would waste precious time if he didn't think this through. He oriented himself to the floor below, picturing where the turbolift hung. Then he quickly walked down the tunnel past the doors until he felt he was close to where the lift would be. He pressed the button marked ACCESS on door B37. The door hissed open and he stepped out onto a small landing.

The turbolift still hung precariously out in the middle of the giant space. If he followed the catwalk, it would bring him close to the part of the shaft that was still intact. He could cut a hole in it with his lightsaber by leaning over the catwalk railing. Then he would have to hoist himself into the shaft and walk a short distance to the turbolift.

If the shaft didn't break free because of his weight . . .

Obi-Wan knew he would have to take the chance. Peering over the catwalk, he could see that Bant hadn't arrived with help. If the service lift tube was out of order, perhaps the comm unit was as well.

Quickly he moved down the catwalk. Massive illumination banks surrounded him. Peering through them, he could see the glint of the lake far below. Even the tallest trees seemed impossibly small from this height.

When he reached the area of the shaft that curved close to the catwalk, Obi-Wan powered up his lightsaber. Carefully and slowly, he carved an opening in the shaft. He did not want the peeled metal to fall back into the shaft itself. Then he returned his lightsaber to his belt.

He climbed over the railing. Now there was nothing between him and the lake hundreds of meters below. He could not hear any noise from the turbolift, but he felt the ripples of distress and fear. He could sense that children were trapped inside.

Obi-Wan slid himself halfway into the shaft. Without letting go of the railing, he tested his weight. The shaft didn't wobble, or make a noise. It would hold him. He eased off the catwalk, ready to spring back if the shaft began to swing. But it didn't move.

He would have to move slowly. If he ran, the vibration could jostle the shaft and it could break free. Obi-Wan closed his mind against the dark lake below, the image of trapped children falling. He began to walk. The shaft was dark, and he activated his lightsaber for illumination. Ahead he could see the bulky form of the turbolift. As he drew closer, he could hear the deep voice of a Jedi caretaker and the occasional murmuring of the children.

His progress was agonizingly slow, but he reached the turbolift wall at last. He tapped on it.

"It's Obi-Wan Kenobi," he called. "I'm in the turbolift shaft."

"It's Ali-Alann," the deep voice said. "I am the children's caretaker."

"How many are inside?"

"Ten children and myself."

"Help is on the way."

Ali-Alann's voice had not a trace of nerves in it. "The repulsorlift engines malfunctioned one by one. Only one holds us. The comm unit is not working. The escape hatch will not open. I don't carry a lightsaber."

Obi-Wan knew what Ali-Alann was telling him. The last repulsorlift engine could go at any time. They were trapped.

"Keep the children away from this wall," Obi-Wan directed him.

Again moving more slowly than he liked, Obi-Wan cut a hole in the turbolift wall. The metal peeled back but did not separate from the lift itself. Good. Obi-Wan held his lightsaber like a torch. The glow revealed the upturned, serious faces of the children and the evident relief on Ali-Alann's face.

"We have to move very slowly," Obi-Wan told Ali-Alann, then shifted to a low voice so that the children would not overhear. "The shaft is precarious. I'm not sure how much weight it can hold."

Ali-Alann nodded. "We'll bring them out one at a time then."

The process was agonizingly slow. The children were all under four years of age. They could walk, of course, but Obi-Wan thought it better to carry them. Ali-Alann handed him the first child, a small human girl who trustingly wound her arms around Obi-Wan's neck.

"What's your name?" he asked.

Her red hair was braided in coils around her head, and her brown eyes were serious. "Honi. I'm almost three."

"Well, Honi-who-is-almost-three, hang on to me."

She pressed her head against his chest. Obi-Wan walked back down the shaft. When he got to the opening, he held Honi against him with one hand and reached out to grab the catwalk railing with the other. It would require perfect balance to make the move to the catwalk.

He heard the sound of footsteps. In another instant Qui-Gon stood across from him on the catwalk. He held out his arms. "I can take the child."

Obi-Wan swung out as Qui-Gon reached and safely passed Honi to him.

"There are nine children left, and Ali-Alann," he said.

"The Masters are below," Qui-Gon told him. "They are using the Force to keep the turbolift aloft."

Now Obi-Wan could feel it: a tremendous wave in the Force, strong and deep. He glanced below. The Council members stood in a ring, their focus on the turbolift.

"But I would not dawdle, just the same," Qui-Gon said dryly as he turned to bring Honi to safety.

Obi-Wan made his way back to the turbolift. One by one, he carried out the children. One by one, he handed them to Qui-Gon. The children were already trained in calmness and the Force. Not one whimpered or cried, although some had to try hard not to. Trust was in their eyes and the relaxed posture of their bodies as they allowed themselves to be carried and handed over a gap to the tiny catwalk hundreds of meters above the lake.

When only two children were left, Ali-Alann carried one to safety while Obi-Wan took the last, a young boy only two years old. Obi-Wan waited while Ali-Alann walked down the shaft. He heard the shaft creak and felt it wobble as Ali-Alann slowly made his way toward the catwalk. The Jedi was tall and strong, with a similar build to Qui-Gon's. Obi-Wan could sense the weakening of the shaft as Ali-Alann moved.

At last he handed over the child and swung himself onto the catwalk. Obi-Wan made the trip for the last time. With every step, he felt the shaft sway. Yet he knew that if he ran, it could break away completely. He handed the child to Qui-Gon and swung himself onto the catwalk. The shaft swayed but did not break. He looked down below and saw the Jedi Masters in a ring, concentrating on the shaft high above their heads.

Jedi Knights had already carried the children downstairs in relays. Obi-Wan followed Ali-Alann and Qui-Gon down the long, winding staircase to the lake level. Sweet relief coursed through him. The children were safe.

He walked behind Qui-Gon to the lakefront where the Masters were waiting. Bant held a child in her arms, talking to him quietly, and Yoda placed a hand on the head of one of the children. The atmosphere was being kept calm so that the children would not be frightened by their experience.

"You did well, children," Mace Windu said, flashing them a rare smile. "The Force was with you."

"And Ali-Alann was there, too," Honi spoke up earnestly. "He told us stories."

Smiling, Mace Windu patted her hair. "Ali-Alann will take you to the dining hall now. But *not* on the turbolift."

The children laughed. They clustered around Ali-Alann, obviously adoring their large, gentle caretaker.

"Well you handled this, Ali-Alann," Yoda told him. The Council members nodded.

"The Force was with us," Ali-Alann repeated. He led the children away.

"And you, young Bant," Mace Windu continued, turning to her. "You are to be commended as well. You stayed calm when you found the comm unit was dead on the lake level. Your speed in getting help was admirable."

"Any of us would have done the same," Bant answered.

"No, Bant," Qui-Gon said warmly. "It was wise to come straight to the Council room. And your calmness in the face of great peril was true to the Jedi way."

Bant colored. "Thank you. My wish was to help the children."

"As you did," Qui-Gon said.

Obi-Wan felt a stab of jealousy and longing. The warmth in Qui-Gon's eyes and voice was unmistakable.

Obi-Wan waited for the Council to notice him. It wasn't as though he had rescued the children in order to win praise. But he couldn't help feeling glad that he had been given an opportunity to come to the aid of the Temple. At least the Council had seen a better side of him.

"As for you, Obi-Wan," Mace Windu said, turning to him, "you are to be thanked for your rescue of the children. You showed quick thinking."

Obi-Wan opened his mouth to answer with humility, as a Jedi should. But Mace Windu kept talking.

"However," he continued, "you also showed that impulsiveness is your flaw. The same flaw that has led us to hesitate about your suitability to be a Jedi. You acted alone. You did not wait for help and direction. You could have endangered the children needlessly. The shaft could have broken free."

"But I tested my weight, and I moved carefully. A — And help was not arriving —" Obi-Wan said, stuttering. He was stunned that the Council had found fault with him.

Mace Windu turned away. Obi-Wan's own voice echoed in his ears, and he realized that he sounded as though he were stammering out excuses. Bant looked at him with compassion.

"Please do not interfere again," Mace Windu said. "The Council will now discuss what is to be done about the shaft. We must close down the wing."

Qui-Gon put his hand on Bant's shoulder. The two followed the Council members from the lake.

Obi-Wan stood, watching them go. He did not think this day could get any worse. Now it had. In the eyes of the Council, he could do nothing right.

And in Qui-Gon's eyes, he was worth nothing at all.

CHAPTER 4

They were too hard on him, Qui-Gon thought as he left Bant and proceeded to his meeting with Yoda. Obi-Wan had acted impulsively, yes — but Qui-Gon would have done the same.

He couldn't interfere with the Council's admonishment, however. And he had come to trust their wisdom in such matters. No doubt it was better for Obi-Wan to reflect on his impulsiveness, since that was what led him to leave the path of the Jedi in the first place. Mace Windu, Yoda, and the Council always had a reason behind their severity. So although he wanted to stay with Obi-Wan, he had left him so that the boy could think about what Mace Windu had said.

Obi-Wan had taken a chance. No doubt about that. Qui-Gon's steps faltered momentarily as he recalled how he felt when he arrived at the lake and realized that Obi-Wan was in the turbolift shaft. A deep sense of dread had pierced him. What if the shaft had broken free before the Masters had arrived? What if Obi-Wan had perished? Qui-Gon's heart stopped at the thought.

His hurried pace resumed. He had learned much over the past weeks about how the heart could surprise you. He was beginning to realize just how intricate and deep the bonds were between him and his former Padawan.

But he must focus on the problem at hand. Whatever needed to be resolved must wait.

Yoda stood in the middle of the empty white space of the safe room in the central tower, where no surveillance could possibly penetrate.

"Confirmed it is by Miro Daroon," he told Qui-Gon. "Sabotage it was. A timing device in the repulsorlift engines, and a bug in the central core that shut down the lift tubes and comm units in the area. Find this person we must, Qui-Gon. After the children now, he is. Strange I find it that Bruck could be involved in such a thing," Yoda brooded.

"The last repulsorlift engine held," Qui-Gon pointed out. "I do not think the turbolift was meant to fall."

Yoda turned to him. "Taunting us, the intruder is? Endangering the lives of babies for a joke?"

"Or there is some other motive," Qui-Gon said. "It's not clear to me yet. At first I thought the petty thefts were designed strictly to irritate and tease. Now I wonder otherwise. The stolen items appear to have served various purposes. The toolbox from the servo-utility unit was most likely used to dismantle the repulsorlift engines. The teacher's meditation robe was used for the intruder to travel about freely, especially in the early morning when most Knights meditate."

"And the fourth year student's sporting gear?" Yoda asked.

"No significance yet," Qui-Gon said. "And then there are the stolen school records. Only students with names A through H. Bruck's last name is Chun. I'm certain the records were stolen to conceal something about him."

Yoda nodded. "Time it will take, to regather information. Something you do not know, Qui-Gon — a sensitive time for the Jedi this is. A secret mission for the Senate we have undertaken. Held in our Jedi treasury is a large shipment of vertex."

Qui-Gon could not keep the surprise from his face. Vertex was a highly valuable mineral. After the raw substance was mined, it was cut into crystals of various shapes for currency. Many worlds used crystalline vertex instead of credits.

"Unprecedented it was, to accept such a shipment," Yoda agreed, noting Qui-Gon's surprise. "Yet the Council thought it best. Two star systems there are, locked in conflict over the shipment. Agree to peace talks they would not, unless a neutral party held the shipment. Almost concluded, the peace agreement is. If word there is that the Temple is vulnerable, war there would be." Yoda's voice dropped in concern. "A large war it would be, Qui-Gon. Many alliances these star systems have."

Qui-Gon digested this information. It often struck him that even while the Temple was a haven, it was connected to the galaxy in so many intricate ways.

"There is no time to waste," he told Yoda. "I will start with Miro Daroon. I must discover how Bruck and this intruder manage to navigate around the Temple without being seen. I'll need to coordinate with Tahl."

Yoda blinked at him. "And Obi-Wan?"

"The Council has ordered Obi-Wan to stay out of this," Qui-Gon answered, surprised.

"Predict I do that the boy will find a way to offer his help again," Yoda said.

"And I should refuse?"

Yoda waved an arm. "Directly involved the boy should not be. But shut him out, I would not."

Qui-Gon smiled grimly as he hurried away. It was contradictory advice, typical of Yoda. Yet the Master's advice somehow always turned out to make perfect sense.

Qui-Gon took a shortcut through the Room of a Thousand Fountains in order to reach the lift tube that would take him directly to the tech center. He walked purposefully through the winding paths, barely noticing his surroundings, intent on the problem at hand.

Then he saw the destroyed footbridge where the attack on Yoda had taken place.

Qui-Gon stopped, his gaze on the splintered bridge, his thoughts suddenly in the past. Years ago, he had a mission to stop a tyrant from taking over a world in the Outer Rim. The tyrant's strategy was based on a simple equation: Disruption + Demoralization + Distraction = Devastation.

That was the pattern, Qui-Gon realized. The thefts had followed the formula. Disruption: the petty thefts disrupted classes and activities. Demoralization: the theft of the Healing Crystals of Fire and the attack on Yoda had caused many students to lose heart. Distraction: the failing of the cooling system, the security breaches, and the destruction of one of the main turbolifts meant that the Jedi had to focus to keep the Temple running. Was the same evil formula working to dismantle the Temple? That tyrant was dead, killed years ago, but had he spread his equation of evil?

Suddenly, Qui-Gon felt a deep disturbance in the Force. It cleaved the air in front of him. The solid rocks seemed to shimmer.

The dark side was here.

The feeling lingered. The fountains continued to flow, the spray from rushing water still cooling his cheeks. He surveyed the area carefully, noting every leaf, every shadow. He saw nothing out of the ordinary.

Yet he knew something was there.

CHAPTER 5

Obi-Wan decided he needed a new comlink. What if something happened in front of his eyes again, and he needed to summon help? Or suppose Qui-Gon or the Council changed their minds and needed him?

It could be wishful thinking, but I don't care, Obi-Wan thought. *I have to think like a Jedi, even if the Council doesn't want me to.*

Instead of heading to his quarters, Obi-Wan started toward the tech center. He was sure that Miro Daroon would let him have a new comlink.

Ahead of him, he saw a familiar figure striding down the hall, munching on a piece of muja fruit as she walked. It was Siri, a fellow student. He didn't know her very well, but he knew she'd been a friend of Bruck's. Maybe if he questioned her, she could come up with a clue about Bruck. He could return to the Council with the information.

He called her name, and she stopped and

turned. The impact of her blue eyes was like a cresting wave. Siri had always been striking, but she hated to have anyone comment on her good looks. She kept her blond hair in a close-cropped style, swept straight off her forehead. The boyish style was probably intended to dim her beauty but instead only enhanced her intelligent eyes and glowing skin.

When she realized who'd called her name, Siri's friendly expression cooled. Obi-Wan wondered why. They had never been friends, but they'd been friendly. Siri was two years younger than Obi-Wan, but her abilities had landed her in Obi-Wan and Bruck's lightsaber class. She had been a worthy opponent. Obi-Wan considered her style athletic and highly focused. Unlike other students, she never got distracted during a duel by emotions such as anger or fear, and she never involved herself in petty rivalries. Privately, Obi-Wan had always thought of her as a little *too* focused. She never seemed to relax or join in the jokes and fun that students enjoyed in their downtime.

"Obi-Wan Kenobi," Siri said flatly. "I heard you were back." She took a bite of fruit.

"Siri, you were a friend of Bruck's," Obi-Wan said urgently. "Did you notice any signs of anger or rebellion in the past few months? Or anything out of the ordinary?"

Siri chewed, staring at him, not answering.

Obi-Wan shifted uncomfortably. He realized too late that these days, being Bruck's friend was not exactly a benefit around the Temple. He had blurted out the question without thinking, eager for answers and mindful of the time pressure. He supposed he should have phrased the question more diplomatically.

While he was trying to think of a better opening, Siri swallowed. She spun the muja fruit in her hand, searching for the next place to bite.

"What's it to you?" she asked.

Her rudeness surprised him, and Obi-Wan struggled not to snap back. "I want to help Qui-Gon find Bruck and the intruder —" he began patiently.

"Wait a second," Siri interrupted. "I thought Qui-Gon Jinn dumped you. And you dumped the Jedi."

Annoyance filled Obi-Wan. "I didn't 'dump' the Jedi," he said irritably. "And as for Qui-Gon, we . . ." Obi-Wan stopped. He didn't owe Siri an explanation! She stood there, chewing on her fruit and staring at him as though he were a lab experiment. "You shouldn't listen to gossip," he told her.

"So why do you want me to gossip about Bruck?" Siri shot back coolly. She took another bite of the muja.

Fuming, Obi-Wan took a breath. The interview wasn't going well, that was for sure. "The Temple is under siege," he said, struggling to keep his voice even. "I'd think you'd want to help."

Siri's cheeks flushed. "I don't have to help you, Obi-Wan. You're not even a Jedi. But for your information, I wasn't a friend of Bruck's. He just used to hang around, trying to copy my lightsaber moves. He knew I was a better fighter than he was. So does the rest of the class. I thought he was a bore. He was always trying to impress me. That about sums up our supposed 'friendship,' all right?"

"All right," Obi-Wan said. "But if you think of anything —"

"And another thing," Siri interrupted, her eyes shooting sparks at him. "I *do* care about the Temple. You're the one who left the Jedi. When you did that, you cast doubt on the commitment of all Padawans, present and future. You made all Jedi Knights question whether we're as committed as we should be. You're almost as bad as Bruck!"

Siri's words hit his cheeks like slaps from an open hand. Color rushed to Obi-Wan's face. Was this what the other students felt? That he had betrayed them?

Obi-Wan hadn't considered before that his action could cast doubt on the commitment of all

Padawans. Faced with a similar situation, would he offer to help someone who had done what he had done?

With every encounter at the Temple, Obi-Wan received a wider picture of the consequences of his decision to stay on Melida/Daan. Now he realized that his action had left a wider pool of ripples than he'd thought.

A decision is yours alone to make. Yet remember you should that you make it also for the silent ones who stand at your shoulder.

How many times had he heard Yoda say that? Now the meaning was so clear that it mocked him with its simplicity. He understood completely what Yoda had meant. He should have understood it before.

Siri seemed to regret her words. Her cheeks flushed almost as deeply as Obi-Wan's.

"If you can think of anything that might help, please see Qui-Gon," Obi-Wan said stiffly.

"I will," Siri murmured. "Obi-Wan —"

But he couldn't bear to hear an apology or an excuse. Siri, he knew, had blurted out exactly what was in her heart.

"I have to go," Obi-Wan interrupted, and hurried away.

CHAPTER 6

Qui-Gon stood in the tech center next to Miro Daroon. Around them curved a blue screen that ran along the wall in the circular room. The screen flashed diagrams of every tunnel, service hallway, catwalk, and duct in the Temple.

At first, the schematic drawings had seemed like a maze to Qui-Gon. But with Miro's help he had soon understood the logic of the diagrams.

But logic hadn't helped to find the intruder. There were dozens of tunnels tall enough for someone Bruck's height to walk upright inside. Ducts were placed conveniently on every floor, giving outlets to every area of the Temple except those under the most severe security restrictions, such as the treasury room.

The problem wasn't discovering a way for the intruder to navigate. The problem was narrowing it down. Qui-Gon had already called the Jedi Knight Tahl, his partner in the investigation, to send out search teams to comb the infrastructure. But that would take time — time they didn't have. He was still hoping for a clue.

Behind them, the door hissed open. Qui-Gon saw Obi-Wan in the reflection on the screen. He saw the boy catch sight of him and pause.

"Have any additional problems cropped up?" Qui-Gon quickly asked Miro.

He wanted Obi-Wan to remain, but couldn't ask him. That would violate the wishes of the Council. But he felt that if he and Miro discussed Temple problems and Qui-Gon didn't ask him to leave, Obi-Wan would stay.

So this is what Yoda meant, Qui-Gon thought.

Miro sighed. He was a tall alien from the planet Piton, thin as a reed, with a high forehead and pale, almost white eyes. Pitons lived underground on their own planet. They had little pigment in their skin that was almost translucent. They were hairless, and Miro wore a cap and tinted eye shields to protect his eyes from glare.

"When I tried to restore power to the service lift tubes in the lake area, the air circulation failed in the north wing. We have to move all the students to temporary quarters in the main building."

In the screen reflection, Qui-Gon saw Obi-Wan studying the diagrams.

"So now two wings of the Temple have been

shut down," Qui-Gon murmured thoughtfully. "You must be very frustrated, Miro."

Miro's mournful face collapsed in a deeper frown than the one he already wore. "Frustrated doesn't cover it, Qui-Gon. I know this system inside and out. But when I fix one problem, three more pop up. It's difficult to keep up. I've never seen such intricate sabotage, not even in hypothetical models. My last resort would be to shut the whole system down to run my own program. That's something I don't want to do."

Qui-Gon felt bothered by this news. Miro was a brilliant, intuitive tech expert. Anyone who could confound him must be a tech genius. Bruck certainly wasn't capable of this. It seemed he was searching for a slippery being with a hatred of the Jedi, a knack for subterfuge, and now a technological wizard as well.

Qui-Gon drew in a quick, startled breath. The knowledge had been in the back of his mind for some time, cold and insidious, like water seeping into the cracks of a boulder. Now it froze into certainty, blasting the rock to smithereens.

"Xanatos," he murmured.

Obi-Wan gave a start. Miro looked at Qui-Gon, shocked. "You think Xanatos is involved?"

"It's possible . . ." Qui-Gon murmured.

The clues had ticked away for a while now. He had sensed a vengeful, personal motive in this operation. Xanatos held an implacable hatred for the Jedi — a hatred that was only surpassed by his hatred for Qui-Gon.

And then there was that feeling he'd had in the Room of a Thousand Fountains . . . could Xanatos have been nearby?

Disruption + Demoralization + Distraction = Devastation. During that mission, Xanatos had been his Padawan. He had been a boy of sixteen. He could have easily remembered the formula.

"I remember him," Miro said quietly. "He was a year behind me. But he was the only Jedi student who was better at constructing tech infrastructure models."

Qui-Gon nodded. The young Jedi student's mind had been what had first attracted Qui-Gon, first made him wonder if he would make a good Padawan.

In that instant, Qui-Gon made a decision. He was not allowed to involve Obi-Wan in the investigation. But things had changed.

He turned and acknowledged Obi-Wan for the first time.

"I need your help," he said.

CHAPTER 7

Obi-Wan stood frozen, surprised at Qui-Gon's words.

"I need to see Tahl and report all this," Qui-Gon said. "I'd like you to come along."

"But the Council —"

"It is my investigation," Qui-Gon said firmly. "You have faced Xanatos before. You could be helpful. So come."

Obi-Wan followed Qui-Gon into the corridor. He walked beside him, feeling a surge of contentment as their footsteps matched in their own rhythm. Not only could he redeem himself by helping the Temple, he would work with Qui-Gon again. Even if he were confined to the fringes of the investigation, he'd take what he could get. It was the first step toward reestablishing the trust between them.

Tahl was checking on the status of the search teams when they arrived. She looked up at them, her lovely face worried. Obi-Wan hadn't seen her since Melida/Daan. She'd been ill after her rescue, thin and drawn. Now her extraordinary green-and-gold striped eyes were sightless, but they gleamed against the dark honey tones of her skin.

"Nothing yet," she said by way of greeting. "Who is with you, Qui-Gon?" She paused. "It's Obi-Wan, isn't it?"

"Yes," Obi-Wan said hesitantly. He was worried about her reaction to his presence. After all, in order to blow up deflection towers for the Young, he'd stolen the transport intended to spirit her off the planet. Would she hold a grudge? But relief flooded him as her face broke into a smile.

"Good. I'm glad." She made a wry face. "You have a knack for rescuing me. It could come in handy. No luck here, I'm afraid."

"I have news," Qui-Gon said crisply. Quickly, he outlined his suspicions about Xanatos.

Obi-Wan could see as Qui-Gon spoke that Tahl was dubious about this supposition. Even as Qui-Gon was finishing, she was slowly shaking her head.

"You're basing much on a leap of logic, my friend," she said.

"It is a fact that Xanatos was known for his technological genius," Qui-Gon argued.

She waved a hand. "As are countless others in the galaxy."

"None as good as a Jedi," Qui-Gon pointed out. "Except one who *was* a Jedi. We must look into Xanatos' recent whereabouts. There could be a clue there."

"I'm not saying you're wrong, Qui-Gon. But what if you are? If we concentrate on one suspect, we could waste time."

The indicator light over Tahl's door went on, announcing a visitor. At the same time, a muted bell sounded. Impatiently, Tahl stabbed at the door access that was at the keyboard on her desk. The door hissed open.

"Yes, who is it?" she asked brusquely.

Obi-Wan was surprised to see that the visitor was Siri.

"I was told by Miro Daroon that Qui-Gon Jinn would be here," Siri said. "Obi-Wan told me to contact you if I remembered anything strange about Bruck."

"Yes?" Qui-Gon asked kindly. "Anything could help."

Siri took a step into the room. "It could be nothing . . . but a few months ago, I had a strange conversation with Bruck. He told me about his father."

Obi-Wan and Qui-Gon exchanged a startled glance. Those who were chosen by the Jedi gave up their birthright. The Temple became their home. That way, their loyalties could not be divided or exploited in any way. They committed themselves to the larger, deeper connection, the Force. It was highly unusual for a Jedi student to mention — or even think of — a parent, especially at Bruck's age.

"I didn't understand how he knew about his father, or why he was so interested," Siri went on. "I asked him why he felt this new compulsion. The Temple is our home, the Jedi are family. These are the bonds we renew day by day. By now they are the strongest things in our lives. But not only was the mention of his father strange, his attitude was as well." Siri hesitated.

"Yes?" Tahl prompted gently.

"It seemed to me that it wasn't so much that he felt a need for a father, or wanted to contact him in any way. He just wanted to brag about him. Bruck discovered — and I don't know how, because he wouldn't say — that his father had become a powerful person on another planet."

"Which planet?" Tahl asked. "Can you remember?"

"One I never heard of," Siri answered. "Telos."

Tahl stiffened. Obi-Wan and Qui-Gon exchanged another glance. Qui-Gon had his proof. Telos was Xanatos' home.

Yet satisfaction did not register on the Jedi's rugged face. Only disquiet.

"Thank you, Siri," Qui-Gon said. "You have been of more help than you know."

"I am glad to hear it." Siri gave Obi-Wan a quick glance, but he couldn't tell if it was a challenge or apology. She left, the door hissing behind her.

"Well, I should know better by now than to doubt you," Tahl said to Qui-Gon. She let out a long breath. "Xanatos."

"No wonder the student records were stolen," Qui-Gon said thoughtfully. "Any changes in the status of students' families are recorded in their files. Somehow, Xanatos got to Bruck through his father. He most likely intrigued the boy, planting longings for power in his head, working on Bruck's anger and aggression until he turned him to the dark side. The same thing," Qui-Gon murmured, "that Xanatos' own father had done to him."

"And most likely Xanatos taught Bruck how to conceal the dark side as well," Obi-Wan added. He remembered during his own meeting with Xanatos how Qui-Gon's powerful enemy could manipulate the truth. His silky manner hid a devious purpose. He had placed doubt in Obi-Wan's mind about Qui-Gon.

"True, Obi-Wan." Qui-Gon nodded. "Bruck

would have to be practiced at concealment. Because he was a senior student, he was given more freedom. That helped him, too."

"So now we know our intruder," Tahl said.

"I suggest we divide the investigation into two parts," Qui-Gon stated. "Obi-Wan and I must discover where Xanatos and Bruck are hiding."

So he would be included! Obi-Wan felt a surge of quiet satisfaction.

"Tahl, you must find out everything you can about Xanatos and Offworld. It will be tricky — he's very secretive. But your investigative powers are a legend around here. Start working your galactic network."

"There's no need to flatter me," Tahl said dryly. "I can hardly crawl around tunnels with you and Obi-Wan."

Qui-Gon paused. Obi-Wan saw concern suddenly etch his features. He wasn't sure why. Qui-Gon often told him he was not connected enough to the living Force. There was something in the exchange between the two friends that had hurt Tahl, and Qui-Gon had just realized it.

Tahl turned her head, her hand almost knocking over a cup near her elbow. Lightning reflexes caused her to catch it before it fell. Her face flushed deeply.

Then Obi-Wan realized what Qui-Gon had

seen. Tahl had only recently lost her sight. She had once been a brilliant warrior. Now she must feel as though she was being shuttled to the sidelines. But Qui-Gon was right. Tahl could not crawl through ducts and look for physical clues.

He watched as Qui-Gon moved closer to Tahl's desk. "Clues are found in many ways, Tahl," Qui-Gon said quietly. "The right information can save a mission more surely than a battle."

Tahl nodded. Obi-Wan could see the struggle on her face. Qui-Gon's fingers brushed her shoulder in a swift, compassionate touch.

"It will be a challenge," he said. "Whatever clues there are will be well buried. Offworld is made up of a pyramid of false companies, phony titles. Their assets are hidden carefully. No one knows where their headquarters is."

Tahl's eyes gleamed. "No one so far," she said.

Obi-Wan noted her new determination. Qui-Gon had done this. He had not dwelt on her dissatisfaction. He had acknowledged it compassionately, then flung out a challenge to engage her.

I have so much to learn from him, Obi-Wan thought. *And it is not only about battles and strategies and the Force. It is about the heart.*

The door hissed open. "Sir Tahl! I am back

from my errand. Here are the extra data sheets you asked for." TooJay, Tahl's navigation droid, hurried into the room.

Tahl raised her eyebrows to let Qui-Gon and Obi-Wan know that she had created the errand to get TooJay out of her hair. The navigation droid was designed to help Tahl, but often was just a source of great aggravation to a person who preferred to do everything herself.

"I'll leave you to your task," Qui-Gon said. "Obi-Wan and I have work to do."

On their way out of the room, they almost collided with Bant, who was rushing through the open door.

"I think I know how Bruck and the intruder are navigating through the Temple!" she cried.

CHAPTER 8

Bant's silver eyes met each of their glances. "I was thinking about all the different attacks," she said eagerly. "They all took place near water. Think about it — Yoda was attacked in the Room of a Thousand Fountains. The turbolift controls are by the lake. And you could reach the tech center itself through the water purification tanks."

Qui-Gon nodded. "A series of water tunnels links all the systems. I saw it on Miro's diagrams, but I didn't think the tunnels were navigable."

"They are," Bant assured him. "I use them. It's against the rules, I know," she added sheepishly. "But if I'm late for a class, it's so much faster for me to swim than walk."

"The sporting gear," Obi-Wan said suddenly. "The kit must have several breathers."

"Good work, Bant," Tahl said approvingly.

"Excellent deduction." Qui-Gon put his hand on Bant's slender shoulder. She smiled shyly.

Jealousy trickled through Obi-Wan. He fought against it. Jealousy was not an appropriate emotion for a Jedi. Yet he couldn't dampen it, or make it go away. Bant had always trailed after him. She'd worshipped him. Now, in the short time he'd been gone, she'd grown up. Her mind was agile and clever, and she wasn't afraid to challenge him.

And Qui-Gon saw how special she was.

Obi-Wan felt a shock as he realized that if Qui-Gon didn't take him back, he most likely would want another Padawan. Was he thinking of Bant?

"Bant, can you show us the tunnel?" Qui-Gon asked. "We'll need a guide."

Bant nodded. "Of course."

"If any trouble crops up, I want you to fade back," Qui-Gon warned. "Don't engage with Xanatos. He is extremely dangerous."

Bant nodded solemnly. Qui-Gon turned to Obi-Wan. "We'll need breathers."

"I brought some," Bant told him. "I thought you'd want to go right away."

"That was quick thinking," Qui-Gon said approvingly.

Obi-Wan trailed after Qui-Gon and Bant. *Now*

I'm the one who is tagging behind her, he thought, entering the turbolift with them. They took the lift to the cordoned-off lake area.

"I found the tunnel entrance when I was exploring the bottom of the lake," Bant explained as they waded into the cool water. "Water is flushed through every twenty minutes past the hour, so I always keep track of time. It's easy to get out in time, or there are plenty of places to climb to when the water flushes through."

She dove under the surface. Obi-Wan followed the trail of her bubbles. Bant was so graceful underwater that she soon pulled ahead. When she realized this, she stopped and waited for them.

They wound through a grotto of underwater rocks. A panel was cleverly hidden in the face of a large boulder. Bant accessed the panel and swam through. Qui-Gon followed, and then Obi-Wan.

They surfaced in a large tunnel of blue tile with a ceiling that curved overhead. The water was clear and clean.

"This services the fountains and reflecting pools in the wing," Bant explained, her voice echoing against the tiled surface. "There are landing platforms every thousand meters or so. Some of them are high enough to conceal someone who wants to hide. I'll stop as we go along."

Qui-Gon nodded. Bant took a breath and dove under the water. They followed.

Obi-Wan followed Bant's waving pink-orange legs through the crystal water. She led them down tunnel after tunnel, curving and twisting throughout the Temple. They stopped at every landing platform to examine it for traces of Xanatos or Bruck. They found nothing.

At last Bant surfaced at a place where a wide main tunnel narrowed and fed into three smaller tunnels.

"This feeds into the water purification tanks," she said as she bobbed. "We've seen everything. I guess I was wrong." Bant looked discouraged. "We should head back."

"It was a good deduction, Bant," Qui-Gon told her kindly. "And we haven't disproved it yet. We didn't find anything. That doesn't mean that Xanatos wasn't here."

Qui-Gon treaded water, surveying the area. "What's that?" he suddenly asked, pointing to a recessed area to one side.

"It's too small to be a landing platform," Bant said. "I think it's a service area for the purification tanks."

Obi-Wan followed Qui-Gon's powerful stroke

toward the recessed area. The Jedi hoisted himself up on a narrow ledge, water streaming down his tunic. Obi-Wan followed, and Bant easily vaulted up behind them.

Qui-Gon worked his way along the ledge. It ran alongside the side tunnel for a time. Then it ended in a sheer wall. From here they could hear the hum of machinery.

"We're close to the purification tanks," Bant said.

"But why would the ledge just end?" Qui-Gon wondered. He bent to examine the curving wall on one side. "Here. There's an access panel," he said. "Bant?"

Bant eased past Obi-Wan. "I see it," she said excitedly. Her fingers ran alongside the edges. She pressed something, and the curved panel slid open.

Qui-Gon stepped through. When Obi-Wan followed, he saw that they were on some sort of service platform that was suspended above the water in the durasteel purification tank. A narrow, tiled staircase led down to the water below.

Qui-Gon strode to a corner. He bent down to examine a servo-tool kit and some items stacked against the wall.

"They were here," he said.

Obi-Wan felt something that began as a whisper, like a soft breath against the back of his neck. The disturbance in the Force was muffled, and he couldn't quite place it. But Qui-Gon looked up, his keen eyes alert. His gaze met Obi-Wan's.

Yes, his eyes seemed to say, as they had said many times when he was his Master. *I feel it, too, Padawan.*

Then the muffled disturbance escalated to a roar. Below them the water parted, and a black form rose. It was Xanatos.

CHAPTER 9

Xanatos was perfectly still, waist-high in deep water, suspended by the Force without kicking or moving his arms. His wet black hair flowed to his shoulders and his sharp blue eyes, as clear and cold as ice crystals, gleamed in the dim light. Watery shadows sent flickering patterns across his black tunic.

Qui-Gon and Obi-Wan had already activated their lightsabers. They stood waiting.

But Xanatos didn't move to engage them. He smiled.

"It took longer than even I imagined for you to figure out it was me," he called mockingly to Qui-Gon. "That noble head of yours can be so thick. Foolishly, I continue to give you credit for some intelligence."

Qui-Gon stood easily, his lightsaber activated but held loosely at his side. He did not appear to be in attack position, but Obi-Wan knew his fighting style well. If Xanatos were to spring, Qui-Gon had only to shift slightly in order to meet the attack.

Qui-Gon didn't answer Xanatos. His face was a study in composure. He didn't appear to have heard Xanatos at all.

Obi-Wan knew they could not attack while Xanatos remained in the water. If they jumped in after him, their lightsabers would short out if the activated lasers came into contact with water. Xanatos knew it, too. Perhaps that was why he taunted Qui-Gon, goading him to attack.

"You don't even answer me?" he called. "Still holding a grudge? What a hard heart you have, Qui-Gon."

"I wasn't aware we were having a conversation," Qui-Gon answered. He moved forward a step. "That was always the way with you, Xanatos — you prefer the sound of your own voice."

Obi-Wan saw a momentary flush on Xanatos' cheeks. Then he laughed. "How tiresome you are, Qui-Gon. Your petty taunts still miss their mark. You never were very clever. And you still rely on children to do your work. You never would have figured out the water tunnels on your own."

Suddenly, he flew through the air in a great leap, propelled by the Force. His black cape streamed water as he activated his lightsaber in the blink of an eye. Obi-Wan was ready, stepping forward even as Xanatos touched down on the platform.

He saw Bant make a running dive off the platform. She was unarmed, and no doubt was swimming for help. She had only waited for Xanatos to move.

Xanatos' red lightsaber crashed against the green glow of Qui-Gon's. The angry buzz echoed through the tunnel. Xanatos had landed to Qui-Gon's left, and Obi-Wan raced to cover the Jedi's flank.

Xanatos was a skilled fighter. His strength was staggering. When Obi-Wan's lightsaber tangled with his, the shock nearly sent him flying backward. It was all he could do to keep his feet. The platform soon grew slick with their wet footprints and the water from their clothes. It was hard for Obi-Wan to keep his footing.

Xanatos was as quick as he was strong, already whirling away from Obi-Wan's attacks to strike at Qui-Gon.

Gradually, Obi-Wan became aware that Qui-Gon had succeeded in manipulating Xanatos, getting him close to the narrow stairs. Xanatos took a step down, then another, as Qui-Gon stepped up the fierceness of his attack. Obi-Wan saw the reason for the strategy. If Xanatos got close enough to the tank, he would have to swing back to gain momentum for his blows. Xanatos would run the risk of shorting out his lightsaber or weakening his attacks.

The strategy could not be obvious, he knew. They had to distract Xanatos with countermoves so that he wouldn't realize how close he was to the water below.

Obi-Wan joined in the attempt, trying to keep Xanatos off-balance while driving him toward the water. The steps were slippery. It was difficult to get enough grounding to lend strength to his blows. He was tiring, but Qui-Gon remained focused, moving gracefully, forcing Xanatos down another step.

As he fought side by side with Qui-Gon, Obi-Wan felt the familiar rhythm pulse between them. The Force was strong, bonding them together as one unit.

Over the sound of the battle, the sizzle of the lightsabers, and his own heavy breathing, Obi-Wan heard a noise. It started as a rumble in the distance. Within seconds, it was a roar.

It was the water flushing the system. A giant tidal wave of foaming water rushed toward them from a conduit in the tank.

"Jump, Obi-Wan," Qui-Gon ordered. Using the Force, they made a simultaneous leap onto the platform above.

Immediately, Obi-Wan whirled to face Xanatos, who was no doubt behind them.

But Xanatos had not leaped to safety. Grinning, he deactivated his lightsaber, then jumped off the step just as the torrent roared through. Within the flicker of an eyelash, he was swept away.

"He'll drown," Obi-Wan said, astonished at Xanatos' action.

"No, he won't," Qui-Gon said grimly, his eyes on the white water. "We shall meet him again."

CHAPTER 10

The battle had not tired Qui-Gon. Obi-Wan could see that it had only fueled his determination to catch Xanatos and defeat him.

"Let's search the area," Qui-Gon told him. "I have a feeling that Xanatos allowed me to maneuver him down the stairs. It was almost too easy."

"He had planned his escape," Obi-Wan suggested.

"Yes," Qui-Gon agreed. "But with Xanatos, there is always a double motive. He was trying to lead us away from something."

Obi-Wan walked to the opposite edge of the platform. "There's a ladder here," he called.

A slender metal ladder was tucked against the wall. It had been hidden by the platform's edge. Qui-Gon and Obi-Wan climbed down. When they were just above the surface of the water, they could hear the sound of falling water ahead.

"It's a spillover," Qui-Gon called back to Obi-Wan. The area ahead was concealed by Qui-Gon's broad back. "And there's a duct here leading to the outside. I think —"

Suddenly, Qui-Gon paused. Holding onto the ladder with one hand, Obi-Wan leaned out to see.

Lashed against the wall was a small airspeeder.

"We've found his escape route," Qui-Gon said with satisfaction.

"Qui-Gon? Obi-Wan?" Bant's worried voice floated out to them.

"Here!" Qui-Gon shouted, and a second later her face appeared over the platform's edge.

"I brought Jedi security," she said. "Are you all right? Where's Xanatos?"

"He escaped," Obi-Wan told her. "He jumped into the water when the tunnel was flushed."

"Let's go back up," Qui-Gon told them. "Security can remove the airspeeder. At least Xanatos will be trapped inside the Temple."

They climbed the ladder back to the platform, and two members of Jedi security went down to take care of the speeder.

"I was so worried," Bant told them. "I hated

to leave you, but I didn't have a lightsaber, and —"

"You did the right thing, Bant," Qui-Gon interrupted kindly. "When instincts are as good as yours, don't question them."

More and more Obi-Wan had to wonder if Qui-Gon was interested in Bant as his next Padawan. It certainly seemed that the Jedi singled her out.

Qui-Gon turned to him. "You fought well, Obi-Wan."

Normally, Obi-Wan would have felt deep satisfaction from Qui-Gon's praise. But now he only wondered if Qui-Gon was merely being nice, preparing him for the day he would be left behind.

Qui-Gon sent Bant back to brief Tahl on what had happened. Obi-Wan wandered off to the edge of the platform where Xanatos had thrown himself into the foaming torrent. He remembered the deep sense of unease he'd felt when Xanatos had risen out of the water, the black form containing a monstrous evil . . .

He'd been wearing a waterproof satchel on his back, Obi-Wan suddenly recalled. Why?

What if it had been no accident that Xanatos had appeared at the platform? What if he'd come to remove the evidence that showed he'd been there?

What if he'd been tipped off? He certainly had managed to stay one step ahead of the Jedi until now. That wasn't easy.

"I think there could be a spy at the Temple," Obi-Wan said slowly, turning back to Qui-Gon. "Xanatos has someone planted there, warning him of our next move. Why else would he have come here with a satchel on his back?"

"Many reasons, I suppose," Qui-Gon said.

"And remember that he said that you had to rely on children to tell you that he was using the tunnels? How did he know that Bant tipped you off?"

Qui-Gon frowned. "I'm not sure about this, Obi-Wan. The only ones who knew we were searching the water tunnels were Bant and Tahl. They are both completely above suspicion. Bant would never do anything to compromise the security of the Temple."

Stung by how quickly Qui-Gon had leaped to Bant's defense, Obi-Wan blurted, "And what about Tahl? Do you trust her so well?"

"With my life," Qui-Gon answered shortly.

"But you haven't seen her in years," Obi-Wan pointed out. "What if Xanatos got to her somehow?"

"No, Obi-Wan," Qui-Gon said curtly. "You are

wrong. I am used to betrayal. I know exactly what it looks like." He gave Obi-Wan a hard look and turned away.

Obi-Wan felt a stab of pain. He knew Qui-Gon was talking about him.

CHAPTER 11

The moment the words left Qui-Gon's mouth, he regretted them. His harshness had arisen more out of his frustration at Xanatos' escape than anything Obi-Wan had said. Yes, the boy had lost his trust. There was no need to torture him by continually reminding him of it. It was behavior unworthy of a Jedi.

It was his own flaw, Qui-Gon realized heavily. He was the one who could not take the leap to trust again. It was not Obi-Wan's fault. It was a combination of Qui-Gon's history and his nature. Although he felt a connection to other beings, he was slow to trust them. Once his trust was given, it was solid. When it shattered, he was at a loss as to how to refashion it again.

His problem. Not Obi-Wan's.

He needed to tell the boy this. The bond between Master and Padawan had to be one of total trust, and he didn't know if he was capable of giving it, even if Obi-Wan was. It wouldn't be fair to Obi-Wan to take him back under those circumstances. It might be better for Obi-Wan to find a new Master.

I will speak to him. When I am sure what it is I want to say.

Suddenly, the lights in the tunnel dimmed to half-power. Obi-Wan and Qui-Gon exchanged a concerned glance. A moment later, Qui-Gon's comlink buzzed. Tahl's crisp voice came through the unit. "We have some developments here."

"I noticed. We'll be right there." Qui-Gon turned to Obi-Wan. He spoke gently to the boy to make up for his harsh words. "I don't think Tahl is in league with Xanatos," he said. "But you could be right about the spy. Let's keep it in mind."

Obi-Wan nodded. The boy was silent as they hurriedly made their way to Tahl's quarters.

Tahl sat at her desk, a pile of data sheets on her lap. "I just spoke to Miro," she told them. "He's been trying to fix the air circulation system in the senior students' wing. When he took the necessary steps, all the lights in the Temple went to half-power. Plus, the refrigeration unit in the dining hall failed. He's working on it."

"The lights are powered down on every floor?" Qui-Gon asked.

Tahl nodded. A ghost of a smile flitted across

her face. "Now we're almost even, Qui-Gon. We both have to work in the dark."

"Not quite even," Qui-Gon said with a smile that was evident in his voice. "You're still wiser than I am."

Tahl grinned. "Speaking of which, that's not the development I was talking about. I found out something about Offworld. Here, I printed it out for you." She handed the data sheets to Qui-Gon.

Qui-Gon stared at the sheets. There were columns of numbers and names of companies. "You're going to have to tell me. You know I'm not good at galactic finance."

"Offworld is not as solvent as they appear," Tahl said, tapping her finger on the desk. "A futile mining operation on an inhospitable planet has drained its resources. Xanatos refused to accept defeat and just kept pouring more and more money into the operation. There's a rumor that he's secretly plundered the treasury on his home planet of Telos."

Qui-Gon stared down at the numbers, which meant nothing to him. The figures weren't important. Tahl's findings were. If Xanatos was close to financial ruin, maybe his motive for storming the Temple had as much to do with money as revenge.

Always a double motive . . .

"The vertex," he said softly.

"Of course," Tahl breathed.

Obi-Wan looked at them, puzzled.

Qui-Gon thought for a moment. Yoda had told him a secret. But if Obi-Wan was to help them, he had to know. He filled Obi-Wan in on the story of the Jedi agreement to guard the vertex for a short time.

"We've been focusing too much on Xanatos' revenge motive," Qui-Gon said. "Xanatos is more complex than that. Why put himself in such danger if all he got out of it was personal satisfaction? But destroying the Temple *and* walking away with a fortune would be worth much more to him."

"The treasury room is one half level below the Council room," Tahl said. "Isn't it strange how the wings have been shut down one after the other? Now everyone has been moved to the central building. This can't be accidental."

"Xanatos is planning something," Qui-Gon brooded. "He hopes to contain us so that it will be easier to destroy us. But how?"

The door hissed open and TooJay walked in, carrying a tray. "I brought your lunch, Sir Tahl," she announced.

"I'm not hungry."

"There is a protein cake, fruit, and —"

"Just put it down," Tahl ordered absently, her mind still on Xanatos.

TooJay set down the tray and began to straighten Tahl's desk.

"Whatever he is planning, it will happen soon," Tahl said.

TooJay moved one set of papers from one side of the desk to the other.

Qui-Gon stood. "Tahl, can TooJay fetch Bant? We need to talk to her."

Tahl turned toward Qui-Gon, a surprised expression on her face. "Bant?"

Qui-Gon spoke in a meaningful tone. "I'll explain when she gets here."

"TooJay, please fetch Bant from the temporary quarters," Tahl ordered.

"I can wait for your lunch tray, sir," TooJay added.

"Now," Tahl said firmly.

"I will return," TooJay said, hurrying out the door.

As soon as the door closed behind the droid, Tahl turned to Qui-Gon. "What was that about?"

"How did you get TooJay?" Qui-Gon asked her.

"I told you, Yoda arranged for it," Tahl answered.

"Did Yoda bring the droid himself?" Qui-Gon persisted.

Tahl nodded. "Why?"

"It was just a few days after you and I arrived

from Melida/Daan," Qui-Gon mused. "Was the droid ever out of your sight?"

Tahl groaned. "Are you kidding? TooJay is always underfoot." Then she frowned. "Except on the second day. I needed TooJay to guide me to the north wing. But I couldn't locate her for several hours. She said she had to attend some kind of indoctrination training. What are you driving at, Qui-Gon?"

Tahl looked mystified, but Obi-Wan saw where Qui-Gon was heading. "The droid appeared at the same time that the thefts began," he told her.

"Are you saying that TooJay is the thief?" Tahl asked. "That droid is pretty conspicuous."

"No, TooJay isn't the thief," Qui-Gon said. He glanced at Obi-Wan. "But I think we could have found our spy."

"We'll have to be sure," Obi-Wan said. "If we could shut TooJay down temporarily —"

"We could find the transmitter," Qui-Gon finished. "We can't have Xanatos know we suspect."

Tahl's mind worked quickly, absorbing Qui-Gon and Obi-Wan's leaps of thought. "How can we shut TooJay down without arousing suspicion?"

Obi-Wan grinned. "That's easy. Just act naturally."

Tahl turned her head toward him. "What do you mean, Obi-Wan?"

"It's obvious that the droid annoys you," Obi-Wan answered. "Pick a fight and shut her down because you've had enough."

Slowly, Tahl smiled. "I've done it before."

"Very smart, Obi-Wan," Qui-Gon approved. "Let's do it when she returns."

Within minutes, TooJay reappeared. "I cannot locate Bant. If I can say this, Sir Tahl, I do not think it advisable for me to be absent. You could need my assistance. For example, there are data sheets on the floor several centimeters from your left foot —"

"I know that," Tahl snapped. "Qui-Gon, those are for you. Why don't you sit here?" She stood, sweeping an arm toward a chair. The tray of food TooJay had brought earlier crashed to the floor. Obi-Wan sprang forward to help, but Qui-Gon held him back.

"Your lunch!" TooJay scurried forward. "It was ten centimeters to your right —"

"Enough, you driveling droid!" Tahl snapped. "If you don't shut your voice activator, I'll shut it for you!"

"But you won't be able to navigate!" TooJay protested.

"I'll be able to think!" Tahl shouted. She

reached forward and deactivated the droid completely.

Silence fell. Tahl grinned. "Was that natural enough for you, Obi-Wan?"

Qui-Gon strode forward and began to examine TooJay. "Here," he said after a moment. "Right in the joint of the pelvic servomotor. A transmitter."

"Does it record and send simultaneously?" Tahl asked.

"Yes," Qui-Gon said. "I would guess that Xanatos has some sort of trigger on his end that alerts him if the conversation is important. He could have programmed several word triggers, like my name, or Yoda's, his, Bruck's — there could be any number of triggers. That way he doesn't have to listen to everything that happens to you — only what he needs." Qui-Gon examined the transmitter. "This unit transmits audio and visuals."

"So Xanatos has known what we were planning all along," Tahl said, sinking back into her chair. "He's been watching our every move. This is bad news."

"Not at all," Qui-Gon said softly. "Now we do not have to chase him. He will come straight to us."

CHAPTER 12

Qui-Gon turned to Obi-Wan. "Obi-Wan, I need you to go to the temporary dormitory. Pick a senior student with your height and build. Then come back here. And be as quick as you can."

Without taking time to respond, Obi-Wan raced out of Tahl's quarters and headed for the lift tube. He reached the level where the students had set up sleeping areas and hastily scanned the crowd. He already knew who he would choose. Not only was his friend Garen Muln his size, but Obi-Wan trusted his abilities as well.

"Obi-Wan! Are you looking for me?" Bant ran forward from a crowd of students who were busy unrolling bedding.

Obi-Wan continued to scan the sea of students. "I'm looking for someone to help Qui-Gon and me," he said.

"But I can help!" Bant's silver eyes shone eagerly. "I'd be glad to help Qui-Gon."

The jealousy that Obi-Wan had tried to smother suddenly leaped inside him. The hurt and longing he'd been feeling turned into something uncontrollable. The open eagerness in Bant's face made him more furious than ever.

"Yes, I'm sure you would," he told Bant savagely. "I'm sure you'd take any opportunity to show Qui-Gon how valuable you are. How much he needs you."

The light in Bant's eyes dimmed. "What do you mean?"

"I mean you want to be Qui-Gon's Padawan," Obi-Wan said fiercely. "It's obvious. You keep trying to impress him. You hang around him all the time."

Bant shook her head. "But I just wanted to help. I'm not trying to be his Padawan. You're his Padawan, Obi-Wan."

"No, I'm not. You made that clear to me. I let him down. So maybe he deserves you, instead."

Bant's eyes filmed over. "That's not so," she whispered.

Obi-Wan caught sight of Garen. He called his name and beckoned him over. "We need your help," he told Garen as his friend came up.

"Obi-Wan —" Bant began.

"I don't have time to talk," Obi-Wan said brusquely.

Bant nodded, her face full of hurt. Quickly, she walked away.

"What did you say to her?" Garen asked him, taking a step toward Bant. "You hurt her feelings."

Obi-Wan grabbed his arm. "You don't have time to go after her now. Qui-Gon needs you."

Obi-Wan led the way out of the dormitory. He felt guilty about his harsh words. Asking for Garen's help in front of Bant was a deliberate snub.

Garen's look of disapproval both irritated him and fueled his guilt. His friend was silent as the lift tube hissed upward toward Tahl's quarters.

After this is over, I'll apologize to Bant, Obi-Wan thought. *I let my jealousy take over. It was wrong. I'll make it right.*

The lights in the hallway outside Tahl's quarters were still at half-power. Obi-Wan saw Qui-Gon standing by Tahl's door, his back to them.

"Qui-Gon, I brought Garen Muln," he called to him.

The tall man turned, and Obi-Wan saw it was Ali-Alann.

"I apologize," Obi-Wan said. "I thought you were Qui-Gon."

Qui-Gon stepped out from Tahl's open doorway. "That was exactly what you were sup-posed to think."

Qui-Gon studied Garen. "You'll do very well," he murmured.

"Qui-Gon, I am happy to help you, but what am I going to be doing?" Ali-Alann asked re-spectfully.

"Not much," Qui-Gon answered. "You have to be me for a short time, that's all. And Garen, you will pose as Obi-Wan."

Garen nodded. Both he and Ali-Alann had caught Qui-Gon's seriousness.

"Obi-Wan and I will record a voice track," Qui-Gon went on. "You will activate it when you're sure that Tahl's personal navigation droid is nearby. Then you'll go on a search for the in-truders. But you will not find them."

"Why not?" Garen asked.

"Because we will," Qui-Gon said, putting a hand on Obi-Wan's shoulder. His eyes glowed fiercely. "We will put an end to this."

Qui-Gon's hand on his shoulder, his steady words, sent a shiver through Obi-Wan. He had been unfair to Bant. If Qui-Gon was encourag-ing to her, it was only because of his goodness. It didn't mean Qui-Gon wanted Bant as a Pada-wan any more than it meant that he still wanted Obi-Wan. It only meant that he was encourag-ing strength where he saw it.

Obi-Wan realized it wasn't Bant who stood between him and Qui-Gon. It was Qui-Gon's own feelings. He had known that. He just didn't want to accept it.

"We'll have to exchange tunics," Qui-Gon said. "Everything they wear and carry must be ours. We can't underestimate Xanatos. The match must be as perfect as possible."

Tahl suddenly came to the door. Her sightless eyes zeroed in on Qui-Gon exactly. Her ability to place people by their voices was exceptional.

"Qui-Gon, we could have a problem," she said. "Bant has disappeared. She knows she's not supposed to roam the Temple without permission."

Garen and Obi-Wan exchanged a glance. They knew why Bant had left without permission.

Just then, Qui-Gon's comlink signaled. He activated it.

"What a pleasure to greet you again, Qui-Gon."

Everyone froze. The mockery that ran through the deep voice alerted even Ali-Alann and Garen that this was Xanatos.

"What do you want?" Qui-Gon asked tersely.

"My transport," Xanatos answered smoothly. "Fully fueled, on the spaceport landing platform. And no one around to follow me."

"Why should I give you this?" Qui-Gon asked scornfully.

"Hmmm. An interesting question. Perhaps because I have bumped into a friend of yours in the water tunnel. I think it might be a good idea if the fish-girl stays with me for awhile. Unless you object."

It took a moment, no more, for Obi-Wan to realize who Xanatos meant. Bant. He had kidnapped Bant.

Qui-Gon squeezed the comlink so hard that Obi-Wan was surprised it didn't shatter. Tahl grabbed the doorframe. Garen took a step forward, as if he could reach through the comlink and grapple with Xanatos. Only Obi-Wan did not move. His blood had turned to ice, his muscles to stone.

"So do we have a deal?" Xanatos asked. "My transport, and I send the girl back to you. I'll give you fifteen minutes. That is all."

"How do I know you have Bant?" Qui-Gon asked.

Seconds later, a firm, high voice came over the comlink. "Qui-Gon, don't do it. I'm fine. I don't want you to —"

Bant's voice was cut off abruptly. The comlink went dead.

CHAPTER 13

Qui-Gon went inside Tahl's quarters to confer with her. Ali-Alann and Garen followed. Obi-Wan still found himself unable to move.

It was as though his body had taken over, refusing to listen to his mind. No matter how forcefully he told his legs to move, they would not. Never before had this happened, not during battle, not even when Cerasi had been killed in front of his eyes.

The words passed through his mind rapidly, like figures streaming across a data screen.

My fault. My fault. Bant will die. She will die. Xanatos is merciless. She will die. And again it will be my fault.

Bant and Cerasi merged in his mind. His grief was a howl inside his body. It tore at his stomach, his throat, and yet he could not let it loose.

The loss of Cerasi rushed through him, as keen as the moment he had seen the life ebb in her crystal green eyes. She was gone to him forever. For the rest of his days, he would think of her, need her, turn to say something to her, decide to contact her . . . and he would never be able to reach her again.

He loved Bant as he had loved Cerasi. How could he have spoken so harshly to her? How could he have suspected the most loving heart he knew of plotting against him? She would never have tried to take his place with Qui-Gon. He knew that as surely as he knew his own name. He had spoken out of bitterness, out of fatigue, out of his own shame, out of everything but truth.

Bant always spoke the truth. What a valuable friend she was.

And he would lose her. He would lose her forever.

My fault.

If Bant died, the grief would destroy him.

He bent over and stared at the floor, his heart racing as though he'd just fought a battle. He gulped down his panic, but he could not make it go away. Instead it rose in his throat again and again, choking him.

He heard footsteps approach him, then pause. He recognized Qui-Gon's step.

No. Don't let him see me this way.

He struggled to compose himself. But the

panic was too real. The fear squeezed his throat, cramped his muscles. He could not move.

He saw Qui-Gon's boots stop in front of him. Then, to his surprise, the large man crouched next to him. His voice was close to his ear.

"It is all right, Obi-Wan," Qui-Gon said gently. "I understand."

Obi-Wan shook his head. Qui-Gon could not possibly understand.

"Never fear your feelings, Obi-Wan," Qui-Gon said. "They can guide you if you control them."

"I — I can't." Obi-Wan forced the words out. How he hated to admit his weakness to Qui-Gon! But he could not lie.

"Yes, you can," Qui-Gon said with the same gentleness. "I know you can. You are a Jedi. You will focus. You will reach your calm center. Do not try to tamp down the fear. Do not let it grip you. If you let it move through you, it will leave you. Breathe."

Obi-Wan breathed. A tiny part of the panic loosened its grip. He breathed again, and felt the fear rise. This time he did not battle it. He pictured it rising on his breath, leaving his body. His muscles loosened slightly.

"We will rescue Bant," Qui-Gon continued. "We will defeat Xanatos. We will bring him down."

The panic was lessening. But not the shame.

"I hurt her." The words were jerky, forced out on a hiccup of air. "I made her run away."

"Ah." Qui-Gon paused. "Did you send her to Xanatos? Speaking sharply to a friend is wrong, Obi-Wan. It is cause for an apology. But it is not cause to be responsible for what happens afterward. Bant knows that. Her kidnapping is not your fault, and she would be the first to say so. She knows she should not use the water tunnels alone."

Obi-Wan kept his eyes on the floor. He grabbed onto Qui-Gon's calmness like a raft. He strove to find it within himself. He knew that Qui-Gon was frantic to find Bant, was full of anxiety to rid the Temple of Xanatos. Yet Qui-Gon crouched next to him, perfectly willing to wait out his panic.

"You want to return to the Jedi," Qui-Gon continued. "Now *be* a Jedi. This is the moment. This is *exactly* the moment when you must. The very worst time is the time you *must* follow the Code. Cast away your doubt. Let the Force flow through you."

Obi-Wan lifted his head and met Qui-Gon's steady gaze. Now he could feel the Force move between them, gather itself and surround them. He knew that together they could defeat Xanatos. He was able to cast doubt aside and believe.

Qui-Gon saw the change in his face. "Are you ready?"

CHAPTER 14

Tahl sent TooJay on an errand while Qui-Gon and Obi-Wan exchanged clothes with Garen and Ali-Alann.

"Your boots are too big," Garen said, clomping around Tahl's quarters.

"No, your boots are too small," Obi-Wan said, wincing.

Qui-Gon and Tahl stood in a corner, speaking softly to Miro Daroon on the comlink. Their voices blended, interrupted, spoke rapidly and crisply as they conferred on strategy, deciding what Qui-Gon and Obi-Wan would say on the voice track.

When Tahl and Qui-Gon signed off, Obi-Wan and Qui-Gon went over what they would say several times. They would need to have the rhythm of natural conversation, Qui-Gon drilled into Obi-Wan. It was perfectly all right to hesitate or interrupt. But the information had to be exact.

The conversation had to be recorded in the hallway. The noise level and ambient sound had to mimic the area where TooJay would overhear. Ali-Alann and Garen stood at opposite ends of the hallway, making sure no one would pass. They also served as lookouts for TooJay.

While these preparations were made, Obi-Wan felt a constant tightening inside himself. Thanks to Qui-Gon, he had driven out his fear. Now his task was to find his center. He was impatient to engage Bruck and Xanatos. Yet impatience was not an ally in battle. It was an enemy. Qui-Gon had drilled that into him many times. He tried to draw on Qui-Gon's composure. The Jedi Knight seemed perfectly unhurried, yet Obi-Wan saw how quickly and surely he moved and spoke. In barely any time at all, everyone was clear on what had to be done and everyone was in position.

Qui-Gon activated the voice track. "We must talk, Obi-Wan. We must move fast. No doubt Xanatos has moved Bant from the water tunnels. We'll begin the search in the north wing of the Temple. Did you get the infrared sensors?"

"I have them here," Obi-Wan replied. "Where will the other search teams be?"

"They'll start at the high floor of the north wing while we begin at the lowest. We'll meet in the middle and then shut down the wing completely and move onto the south wing. We'll trap them eventually."

"I don't know why we have to leave Xanatos' transport on the landing platform," Obi-Wan protested. "Why should we give him what he wants?"

"Because he might be checking to be sure that we do. We can't endanger Bant. Patience, Obi-Wan. Xanatos will never reach the transport."

"I can't help it," Obi-Wan said fiercely, making his voice rise. "I want to fight them!"

Qui-Gon had directed Obi-Wan to seem impatient. He wanted Xanatos to think the boy was close to the edge of his control. It could give them an advantage in the coming battle if Xanatos underestimated Obi-Wan.

"You must have control," Qui-Gon said sternly. "Now, as we search, remember that Miro will be shutting down the power system. We can't run the risk of other systems failing while we search. Miro will have to shut down the system in order to run a program to find all the bugs."

"Will we lose power completely?" Obi-Wan asked.

"Yes. Miro will have to shut down water systems, communications, power stations, and last of all, security. The turnoff will last for twelve minutes. Then Miro will turn the system back on, beginning with security. It's a necessary risk. Now come. Let's head for the north wing."

Qui-Gon and Obi-Wan walked off toward the lift tube. As soon as they turned the corner, Qui-Gon deactivated the voice track.

He handed it to Ali-Alann and Garen. In a few moments, Tahl would summon TooJay. Ali-Alann and Garen would impersonate Qui-Gon and Obi-Wan and transmit the conversation while TooJay was within earshot. This would give Obi-Wan and Qui-Gon time to position themselves to ambush Xanatos.

Qui-Gon was counting on the fact that Xanatos would be monitoring closely, since he would want to know if his demand would be met. Thanks to the transmitted conversation, he would think he had a clear field.

"You two must seem to follow through on the plan," Qui-Gon directed Ali-Alann and Garen. "Start searching the north wing. Try to stay in ill-lighted areas, just in case Xanatos or Bruck checks to make sure."

Ali-Alann and Garen nodded.

"And what am I to do, Qui-Gon?" Tahl asked softly.

"Your work is done, my friend," Qui-Gon said. "Now it is up to me and Obi-Wan."

"May the Force be with you," Tahl murmured.

"May it be with us all," Qui-Gon quietly replied. He signaled to Obi-Wan, and they headed for the lift tube.

"Where are we going?" Obi-Wan asked.

"To Xanatos' ultimate destination," Qui-Gon answered. "Everything he's done has led to this. Capturing Bant was a bonus — he can now use her as leverage to get his transport back. He knew Miro would eventually have to shut down the entire power core, including the security system. In those precious minutes when security is down, Xanatos is planning to strike."

Of course! "He's going after the vertex in the security chamber," Obi-Wan said.

"And we will be waiting," Qui-Gon replied grimly.

CHAPTER 15

The security chamber was built like a strong-box. It could not be reached by turbolift, only by a short stairway down from the Jedi Council room itself. Access was limited to Jedi Council members, who underwent a retinal scan to enter. Approval had to be received and coded into the central system.

Ali-Alann and Garen's impersonation had given them time to arrange the ambush. Yoda arranged for Qui-Gon and Obi-Wan to enter before security shut down. The hallway outside the chamber was narrow and dark, the lights at half-power.

"Three minutes until Miro shuts down the power," Qui-Gon told Obi-Wan softly. "Xanatos and Bruck will come through one of the air ducts. Do not wait to engage them. Surprise is key. But don't activate your lightsaber too early or the glow will alert them that someone is here."

Obi-Wan nodded. He gripped his lightsaber, keeping his eyes on the ceiling above. The minutes slid by slowly. The unventilated air caused him to perspire. His fingers slipped on the lightsaber hilt. Quickly, he wiped his palm on his tunic.

He tried to summon up Qui-Gon's calm, but it slipped by him. He did not know why he was having such trouble with his composure. Every nerve was on fire. All he could think of was Bant. Was she alive or dead?

The thought of Bant sent panic shooting through him again. Obi-Wan bit down against it. They would save Bant. They would defeat Xanatos. Their enemy was not invincible. He trusted Qui-Gon's strength and cleverness.

Suddenly, the lights went out. Even though Obi-Wan knew this would happen when Miro shut down the central power core, it still made him start. He wrenched his mind to stillness.

A slight noise overhead alerted him that someone was now traveling in the duct system. Qui-Gon kept his eyes trained on the duct closest to the treasury door.

Moments later, the grate slid open. Xanatos and Bruck somersaulted through, both dressed in black, blending into the darkness. The only gleam of light was of Bruck's white ponytail and Xanatos' pale skin.

Obi-Wan and Qui-Gon moved as one. They sprang forward, lightsabers activated.

The surprise on Xanatos' face was gratifying. He gave a strangled cry of rage and sprang back, his hand reaching for his lightsaber.

Bruck was not as quick. He stumbled back, fumbling. The hilt of his lightsaber was in his hand when Qui-Gon, with a delicate touch, knocked it away without touching Bruck's skin. He did not want to harm the boy, just capture him.

Obi-Wan sprang toward Xanatos as Qui-Gon came at him on the other side.

But this time Xanatos surprised them. Instead of trying to elude them, he leaped forward and grabbed Bruck. He held his glowing red lightsaber against the boy's neck.

"Don't come any closer," he said, his eyes snapping a challenge. "You know I'll do it, Qui-Gon."

"Xanatos?" Bruck's eyes wobbled in fear.

"Be quiet," Xanatos snapped. "Now I have two hostages, Qui-Gon," he continued. "Do you want to sacrifice two young lives?"

Qui-Gon made a subtle movement toward Obi-Wan. Obi-Wan felt the Force surge. Qui-Gon was reaching out to him, trying to tell him something. But what?

If your plan is good, there is no reason to abandon it.

Obi-Wan remembered that Qui-Gon had wanted him to seem impatient, close to the edge of control. Xanatos would not look at him as a threat.

"You're not going to let him get away with this, are you?" Obi-Wan shouted, pumping desperation in his voice. "I don't care about Bruck! Let's charge him!"

"The boy is ruthless, Qui-Gon," Xanatos purred. "Did he learn this from you?"

With a cry, Obi-Wan started toward Xanatos. At the same time, Qui-Gon sprang forward. Xanatos gave Bruck a violent shove away from him, trying to use the boy to block Obi-Wan's advance. At the same time, he stepped forward to meet Qui-Gon's first strike.

Bruck dropped to the floor and scrambled for his lightsaber. Obi-Wan leaped to prevent it, but Bruck grasped it, rolled away, and sprang to his feet.

"Make sure she is dead!" Xanatos hissed at Bruck. "Now!"

Bruck took off toward the end of the hallway.

"After him!" Qui-Gon roared to Obi-Wan.

Obi-Wan raced to catch up to Bruck, but Xanatos stepped to the side and made a diving sweep at him. Obi-Wan parried the violent blow, but it drove him backward. He slashed at Xanatos, but Xanatos blocked his every move while twisting to evade Qui-Gon's attack.

Grimly, Qui-Gon stepped up his pace, going after Xanatos again and again, so relentlessly that Obi-Wan was free to maneuver.

He didn't want to leave Qui-Gon alone with Xanatos. But he had to stop Bruck. It was an impossible choice, but he had to make it.

Leaving Qui-Gon behind, Obi-Wan took off to save Bant.

CHAPTER 16

Qui-Gon felt the dark surge of Xanatos' anger charge the air. He did not meet it with his own.

Once he had hated Xanatos, but he could not exist with hate and continue to be a Jedi. He did not hate his enemy. He wished to stop him. There was a difference. He knew Xanatos wanted him to use hate and anger. Xanatos wanted more than anything to prove that Qui-Gon Jinn could violate the Jedi Code. That would be his victory.

Qui-Gon found his core of purpose and stillness even as he vaulted, somersaulted, came at Xanatos from one approach, then another. His will collided with that of his former apprentice.

Xanatos flipped backward twice, then changed hands and came at Qui-Gon from a different angle. This was a new skill. Now Xanatos fought with two hands. Qui-Gon would have to be alert for a sudden change in attack. He parried Xanatos' blow with a backhanded sweep, then whirled to jab an uppercut toward the chin. Xanatos stepped back, anticipating the move. But Qui-Gon was already reversing. His next blow missed Xanatos by a hair. He saw the displeasure in his eyes.

Xanatos turned and ran. Qui-Gon gave pursuit, running swiftly up the staircase and bursting into the Jedi Council room.

The Force warned him to duck, and he rolled away to his left. A small table smashed into the wall behind him, propelled by the Force. Qui-Gon ducked as a viewscreen followed, smashing as it hit the wall behind his head. He sprang forward, descending on Xanatos with a lightning-fast series of lunges.

"Your age is slowing you down, Qui-Gon," Xanatos panted. "Five years ago you would have dispatched me inside the security chamber. Now I am faster than you."

"No," Qui-Gon said as their lightsabers clashed. "You just talk more."

He circled Xanatos, looking for an opening. Xanatos kept moving, keeping the Council chairs between them. Using the Force, Xanatos caused one to slide away and smash against the wall. Then he pounced.

Their battle assumed a new ferocity. Again

and again their lightsabers tangled as each tried to gain the advantage.

"Give up, Qui-Gon," Xanatos growled. "I will outlast you. I will kill you here, then steal the vertex. Your precious Jedi will have to go on without you."

Qui-Gon blocked a sweeping blow. "Your small mistakes have always been your downfall."

"I . . . don't . . . make . . . mistakes." Xanatos grunted out the words as he took an involuntary step backward under the fury of Qui-Gon's assault.

"Your footwork betrays you," Qui-Gon answered, pressing his advantage with a slashing blow. "You don't realize how you let me know your next move. Notice how your body is leaning just slightly. You're placing more weight on the ball of your left foot. You're going to move left."

Xanatos shifted his balance, and Qui-Gon, already anticipating his reaction, drove forward. Xanatos nearly dropped his lightsaber as he slammed against the wall.

Ready to push his advantage, Qui-Gon leaped after him. But Xanatos switched hands again, parrying Qui-Gon's blow as he leaped across the room. He landed on a table close to the window. Gripping his lightsaber, he cut a hole in the window that overlooked the tall towers of Coruscant.

The window peeled back. Keeping his eyes on Qui-Gon, Xanatos smiled.

"You will never defeat me, Qui-Gon Jinn. That is your curse."

Then he leaped out into thin air.

CHAPTER 17

Since the turbolifts weren't operational, Obi-Wan had to race behind Bruck down hallways and stairs. The sound of Bruck's heavy footsteps alerted him to the boy's direction. Bruck had never been light on his feet.

Soon, Obi-Wan guessed where Bruck was heading — the Room of a Thousand Fountains. Where better to hide Bant than underwater?

He ducked into the room. Immediately, he spotted Bruck running along one of the trails that twisted through the greenery. Obi-Wan ran as silently as he could, hoping to surprise Bruck from behind.

But an instant before Obi-Wan reached him, Bruck stepped off the path and reversed direction. He had learned cunning from Xanatos.

The Force warned Obi-Wan of the attack a split second before, or he would have run into the end of Bruck's lightsaber. Bruck came at him with a two-handed sweep.

Obi-Wan had time for a flashpoint of unreality, as though he were in a dream. His old adversary advanced, a light of anger and rivalry in his eyes. Everything was so familiar — Bruck's aggressive stance, his small, angry eyes, the way his fingers gripped the hilt of the lightsaber.

But this isn't training. It's real. He wants to kill me.

Obi-Wan deflected the blow and whirled to take the offensive. But Bruck had gained in strength as well as strategy. He blocked Obi-Wan's blow and struck again.

"I've learned well, haven't I?" he asked, his pale blue eyes fierce. "Xanatos showed me what true power is. The Jedi will regret that they held me back!"

"They never held you back," Obi-Wan said, parrying Bruck's strike. He stayed on the defensive, waiting to turn into the aggressor. If he kept Bruck talking, perhaps he could spot Bant. While he parried and struck, his eyes darted around, searching for a glimpse of her under the still surfaces of the pools that surrounded him.

"No one chose me as Padawan!" Bruck cried,

grunting as he swung a brutal blow toward Obi-Wan's legs.

Obi-Wan danced backward. "Then you were not ready."

"I was ready!" Bruck screamed. Then his expression grew crafty. "More ready than you, Obi-Wan. You're the one who disgraced the order."

Obi-Wan knew that Bruck was trying to get him to lose his temper. But the words still hit their mark. His next blow had anger behind it. He saw Bruck's satisfied smile.

Yes, Bruck had learned well from Xanatos.

"I was always better than you," Bruck taunted him. "Now I am even stronger."

But Obi-Wan knew that he, too, was stronger. Thanks to Qui-Gon he was a smarter fighter, cooler, with better strategy.

As long as I don't give in to my anger.

Obi-Wan remembered how Qui-Gon had pointed out that in the battle on the platform, Xanatos had subtly kept them away from what he was trying to conceal: the airspeeder. Now Obi-Wan wondered if the apprentice had learned from the Master: was Bruck pushing him back slowly in order to keep him away from seeing Bant?

With a great leap, Obi-Wan suddenly launched

an offensive. His furious blows sent Bruck backward, and he kept up the assault, driving him down the path. Sweat poured from his body as he swung the lightsaber in a ceaseless motion, attacking Bruck from all sides.

The highest waterfall loomed ahead. Normally the cascading water flowed into a deep pool, but since Miro had turned off all systems, the waterfall was dry.

But the pool was not. Obi-Wan felt his heart stop as he glimpsed a flash of a lighter blue underneath the deep sapphire of the water. Bant's tunic! His fear threatened to choke him, but he willed it to calm. He drove Bruck before him relentlessly until they reached the edge of the pool.

Bant lay on the bottom. Her ankle was securely chained to a heavy anchor. Obi-Wan felt relief course through him as tiny bubbles rose to the surface of the water. She was still alive.

Bant could last underwater for long periods of time, but she needed oxygen to breathe. How long had she been under?

"She doesn't look too good, does she?" Bruck remarked as he took advantage of Obi-Wan's distraction to administer a two-handed blow toward his midsection.

Obi-Wan raised his lightsaber and deflected the blow. As he staggered from the impact, he screamed Bant's name, calling on the Force to help him reach her.

Her eyelids opened slowly. She blinked. But she seemed to barely register his presence. Her eyes closed again.

Hold on, Bant!

But Obi-Wan did not feel an answer. Her living Force was ebbing. He could feel it. Bant would die.

"That's right, Obi-Wan," Bruck taunted him. "Bant is dying. I won't have to do a thing. I'll just make you watch it. We would have freed her if we got the treasure. But another person will die because of you. Right in front of your eyes. Just like your friend Cerasi. I overheard the other Jedi talk about how you failed *her.*"

At the sound of Cerasi's name, something shattered inside Obi-Wan. The composure he'd fought for was gone now. He attacked Bruck in a fury, not caring about strategy or finesse.

Startled, Bruck backed up the hill that formed the waterfall. It was a rocky slope, the footing treacherous. Ruthlessly, Obi-Wan pressed Bruck, driving him up, keeping him off-balance. Their lightsabers tangled. Obi-Wan's arm muscles ached as he swung with all his might with each stroke. He felt clumsy in Garen's too-small boots.

Bruck reached the top of the hill. He took the

opportunity to plant his feet and swing down at Obi-Wan, aiming for his chest. Obi-Wan twisted as he parried the blow. His foot slipped on the mossy rocks and he landed on one knee. Pain sliced through him, followed by fear.

If he lost this battle, Bant would die.

Still on one knee, Obi-Wan managed to deflect Bruck's thrusts. But he had allowed anger to pierce his heart — deadly for such an intense battle.

The muscle weakness he had felt outside Tahl's quarters returned. He could barely keep the lightsaber moving in order to counteract Bruck's blows. He tried to use the Force again, but it proved as slippery as the moss-covered rocks.

"Good move, *Oafy*-Wan," Bruck sneered.

Bruck had given him that nickname when they were students in the Temple, making fun of his growing legs and his occasional misstep during training.

At the memory of Bruck's cruelty, a sudden passion for vengeance rose in Obi-Wan. Bruck's cruelty had once been petty. Now it was dangerous. Xanatos had made Bruck a killer.

Boiling anger blurred his vision. He hated Bruck as he had hated no living creature. Anger drove out the Force completely, leaving him in a vacuum that he filled with his rage. The rage united with his fear and panic and created a dark cloud that threatened to overtake him completely.

Bruck saw the change in his eyes. His own pale blue eyes flashed with cruel satisfaction. He planted both hands on the hilt of the light-saber and raised it high.

In that split second, Obi-Wan saw the seeds of his own defeat.

This is the moment. The very worst time is the time you must follow the Code.

Cast away your doubt, Padawan. Let the Force enter you.

Obi-Wan raised his saber. He let his anger and fear move through him, exhaling them in a breath. He reached inside and found his center of calm.

Bruck's lightsaber came down, and he blocked it. But his diversion had cost him. He struggled to the lip of the hill and gained it just as Bruck's next blow fell. Obi-Wan parried the strike, but did not have the balance to counterattack. It didn't matter. He had regained his calm. He could regain his footing. He knew now that he could defeat Bruck.

But Bruck was equally certain of victory. Obi-Wan's fall and his unsteady footwork had convinced him that the battle was his. Bruck's flaw had always been overconfidence when he thought he was on the verge of winning. . . .

Obi-Wan circled around Bruck, forming a new strategy. He bounded from a rock and flipped over Bruck so that he was behind him. He just needed a moment to check his chrono so that Bruck would not notice.

Miro was shutting down the system for twelve minutes. He had about eleven seconds until Miro began powering up the different systems, one by one. First, security. Then the water systems would resume.

Obi-Wan moved forward, pushing Bruck back toward the dry bed of the waterfall. He made sure to continue to block Bruck's blows and retaliate, but weakened his stroke slightly. He still wanted Bruck overconfident.

"Getting tired, Oafy-Wan? Don't worry. It won't be long before I finish you off."

Out of the corner of his eye, Obi-Wan saw the red security light beam on the service console. The water would be next.

Bruck's ponytail whipped around as he whirled, attacking Obi-Wan from the left. Instead of blocking the blow, Obi-Wan stepped aside so that Bruck's momentum would send him into the dry waterfall bed.

He heard a distant roar. If Bruck heard it, he

did not understand its significance. His entire being was focused on his anger and his lust for victory.

The water gushed from the hidden pipes and spilled out in a torrent. Obi-Wan had timed his counterattack, and Bruck found himself surrounded by water. He was barely able to keep his footing, but he swung his lightsaber back to aim another blow at Obi-Wan . . .

And hit the water with the laser. With a fizzing sound, the saber shorted out.

"That's it, Bruck," Obi-Wan said. "Give up."

"Never!" Bruck yelled fiercely, hate still in his eyes. Bruck's face contorted in a frenzy of frustrated rage. He leaned down to pick up a weapon to throw at Obi-Wan, any of the rocks that lined the bed. But the water pulled at him, and he slipped on the mossy rocks. He lost his footing and stumbled back to the very edge of the waterfall. He teetered on the edge for an instant, his eyes wide with disbelief and panic.

In one fluid motion, Obi-Wan deactivated his lightsaber and leaped forward. He reached out a hand, ready to pull Bruck to safety.

But it was too late. Bruck's panic sent his arms windmilling, further unsettling his balance. Obi-Wan felt Bruck's fingertips brush his as his opponent tumbled backward into thin air.

Obi-Wan stepped forward and grimaced as

he saw Bruck's body hit a rock and bounce, then hit another. He landed on the dry grass beside the waterfall. His head lay at an awkward angle, and he was still.

Obi-Wan gathered the Force to him and dove off the top of the falls.

He landed clear of the rocks, and pushed himself upward through the cool water. He swam quickly to the bank and vaulted out onto the grass. He felt for Bruck's vital signs.

Bruck was dead. Obi-Wan guessed that he had died instantly. His neck was broken.

He did not have time to wonder how he felt about that. There was Bant to save. Obi-Wan felt in the interior pocket of Bruck's tunic, hoping to find a key to unlock Bant's chains. Surely Xanatos had given Bruck the means to free Bant as well as let her die.

His fingers closed around a small durasteel square with holes drilled into it. It had to be the key.

Taking a deep breath, he dove into the pool. He swam down toward Bant. He grabbed the chain and fitted the durasteel square into the lock. The chain fell free.

Obi-Wan scooped up Bant and hugged her to his chest. She felt as insubstantial as a handful of snow.

He exploded above the water, gulping air, and

swam to the bank. He waded out and carefully lay Bant on the grass.

Her eyes fluttered open. "Breathe," he urged.

She took a ragged breath, then another. Color began to return to her cheeks.

Obi-Wan laid his head against the top of hers. He kept his arm around her. His warm tears mingled with the cold moisture on her skin.

"I'm so sorry," he told her. "I'm so sorry. This was my fault."

Bant coughed. "Don't," she said.

Don't what? Hold her?

"No . . . need," she forced out.

Things were not resolved between them. There was so much he needed to say. But he could not leave Qui-Gon to fight Xanatos alone any longer.

"I have to help Qui-Gon," he said. "Will you be all right?"

Bant's breathing was easier, and her nod was strong. "I'm fine. Go. You're his Padawan. He needs you."

CHAPTER 18

Qui-Gon moved fast. He leaped out the broken window after Xanatos. He knew the same thing Xanatos did — that outside, a narrow ledge ran underneath the windows.

He used the Force to propel his leap and guide him to the ledge. Xanatos was already moving away from him. Qui-Gon guessed he was heading around to the south, where the landing platform was, fifteen stories below.

Qui-Gon could see the spires and towers of Coruscant. Airspeeders and air transports buzzed above and below him. An air taxi sailed by. One of its passengers looked out, then did a double take when he saw the two men on the ledge hundreds of kilometers in the air.

The wind was powerful up there, rising in gusts that were strong enough to make Qui-Gon stagger. He hung onto the sill above his head until a gust passed, then pressed on.

Xanatos was moving quickly, but Qui-Gon knew he could catch up to him.

Xanatos looked back and grinned. The wind whipped his black hair, and his blazing blue eyes looked deranged. The wind was dying down. Qui-Gon moved quickly, almost running.

He caught up to Xanatos before they were above the landing platform. He could not let Xanatos move much farther in that direction.

Qui-Gon activated his lightsaber and attacked. This was the moment. This was his stand. He would kill Xanatos here. Not from anger. From the certainty that this evil had to be stopped.

They fought with concentrated ferocity, each blow designed to cause the other to stagger and fall. Balance was tricky on the narrow ledge. Wide blows could only come from one side. Follow-through was difficult. Still Qui-Gon adapted his style to fit the area. He used short jabs, sometimes falling on one knee to come at Xanatos from below. He felt the Force swirl around him, strong and sure, aiding his instincts, telling him where Xanatos would move next and how. He blocked each blow and came back stronger. He sensed that Xanatos was on the edge of desperation, though his former apprentice would never let him see it.

"Haven't you forgotten something, Qui-Gon?" Xanatos called to him over the screaming wind.

"The last part of that takeover equation. Devastation."

"You must be tiring, Xanatos," Qui-Gon said. "That's when you begin your taunts." He gritted his teeth as he slammed a blow toward Xanatos' shoulder.

Xanatos blocked it. "Your precious Temple is doomed!" he shouted. "When that idiot Miro Daroon powers up the last link in the system, the whole fusion furnace will blow. The Temple will implode. Did you really think I'd allow the Jedi to follow me?"

Qui-Gon staggered both from surprise and an unexpected short strike from Xanatos' left. *Was he telling the truth?* Desperately, Qui-Gon realized there was no way for him to know.

He attacked furiously, delivering a wide arm sweep from the left. The two lightsabers tangled. For an instant, their faces were very close. Xanatos' eyes burned with a strange light. The pale half-circle scar on his cheek gleamed.

"What you revere can destroy you." His voice was soft, yet Qui-Gon caught every word. "Haven't you learned that yet?"

Above him, Qui-Gon saw the lights of the Council room flicker. After the lights, Miro would power up the communications system. Then the repulsorlift engines for the turbolifts throughout the complex. The air circulation would be last.

Qui-Gon calculated that he had only three minutes before the explosion. Maybe four. If Xanatos was telling the truth . . .

"You can't be sure, can you, Qui-Gon?" Xanatos sneered. "Will you allow your precious Padawan to die just to kill me? He tried to get away from you once. Why don't you get rid of him for good?"

Qui-Gon hesitated, his lightsaber held in attack position. He knew he could defeat Xanatos. But how long would it take?

In that split second, Xanatos glanced below. An air taxi flew twenty meters underneath the ledge. Qui-Gon sprang forward, but Xanatos stepped off the ledge. He landed on the air taxi. Qui-Gon saw the surprised driver's look of panic as Xanatos calmly lifted him out of the seat and pushed him out into midair.

Qui-Gon had less than a second to decide. He could make the jump. He could land on the taxi. He could grapple with Xanatos. He could end this once and for all.

The second passed. Xanatos roared away. Helpless rage surged in Qui-Gon even as he deactivated his lightsaber and raced for the opening in the window.

Qui-Gon jumped inside and ran, accessing his comlink as he moved. He tried to reach Miro, but the communication fields weren't fully functioning.

He was halfway to the turbolift before he realized that it wouldn't be operating. Qui-Gon's frustration was turning to panic. How could he reach the tech center in time?

Suddenly, Obi-Wan burst into the hallway from the stairs.

"He's rigged the Temple to implode," Qui-Gon told him. "We have to get to the tech center."

Obi-Wan was already moving. "Follow me."

CHAPTER 19

As they raced down the hall, Qui-Gon asked tersely, "Bant?"

"She's fine," Obi-Wan said shortly. "Bruck is dead."

A pall had settled over Obi-Wan's face. He would need to talk about this later, Qui-Gon knew.

"I studied the diagrams," Obi-Wan told him, changing the subject as they turned the corner. "I can get us there faster through the infrastructure of the building."

Obi-Wan leaped and kicked open a duct overhead. Qui-Gon noticed that he was barefoot. "Garen's boots slowed me down," he explained as he swung himself in. Qui-Gon followed. They crawled down a short length of an air circulation shaft and came to a service panel. Obi-Wan accessed it. It slid open and he climbed in.

It was a tight fit, but Qui-Gon made it. Here he

could stand upright. They were on a catwalk, surrounded by machinery.

Qui-Gon heard a slow whining noise. "The repulsorlift engines are starting up," he said.

"This way." Obi-Wan ran down the catwalk. He came to a vertical ladder and began to scramble down. Quickly, Qui-Gon followed.

The ladder left them at a service door. Obi-Wan pushed through. They were now ten levels down.

"There's a back stairway to the right," Obi-Wan said as he raced down the hallway with Qui-Gon beside him. "It will bring us to the horizontal tube that is used to transport food from the dining hall to the med unit."

They came to the tube. Obi-Wan gestured for Qui-Gon to go inside. Qui-Gon crammed himself into the small space. Obi-Wan squeezed in next to him. Then he hurriedly set the controls. In seconds, they were sucked down the tube on a moving ramp. At the end, Obi-Wan kicked open the door.

They spilled out in one of the resting rooms in the med unit. Qui-Gon knew it was on the same level as the tech center. But he also knew that a shaft separated the two wings.

Qui-Gon checked his chrono. "We have about one minute," he told Obi-Wan.

Obi-Wan's face was streaked with sweat. "The gas duct." He turned and ran.

Qui-Gon followed. Out the window he could see that across the shaft ran an air-systems duct. "Where does it come out?"

"Right where we want it to," Obi-Wan said, locking his fingers in the grate and prying it off. He kicked it aside and scrambled inside the duct. "It's the gas transport system for the freezer containers used to store med supplies."

Qui-Gon squeezed into the opening. The duct wasn't high enough for him to stand. He followed closely behind Obi-Wan as they crawled rapidly down the tunnel.

"Obi-Wan, what happens if Miro tests the gas transport system when he powers up the air ducts?" Qui-Gon asked.

There was a pause. "I'm not sure," Obi-Wan answered.

Qui-Gon knew that the gas pumped into molten carbonite was toxic, but decided to keep the information to himself. He didn't need to tell Obi-Wan. The boy had caught the implication and scrambled even faster down the tunnel.

Thirty seconds. Qui-Gon tried to move fluidly, gracefully. He was a big man, and wasn't normally fast on his hands and knees in a confined space. He felt the Force surrounding Obi-Wan in front of him, and it seemed to vibrate around them in the enclosed space, giving them strength and agility.

Qui-Gon saw a fractured beam of light ahead. They were approaching the grate.

Obi-Wan blasted through the opening so fast he seemed just a streak to Qui-Gon. Qui-Gon swung himself out. Miro was standing at the console, his fingers flying on the keys.

"Stop!" Obi-Wan and Qui-Gon yelled together.

"Don't activate the air circulation system," Qui-Gon warned. "It's booby-trapped."

It didn't seem possible that Miro's translucent skin could pale. But for a moment he seemed to shimmer like a ghost. He jerked his hand back from the console.

"We have to find the bug," Qui-Gon said, striding toward the console.

Miro punched in a code, and the blue screen that surrounded them filled with numbers and graphs. "I ran a complete bug check when the system was powered down," he said. "Nothing came up. There's no program in the system anymore except for mine. Are you sure about this, Qui-Gon?"

"No," Qui-Gon said reluctantly. "Xanatos could have lied. But can we take the chance?"

"I can run the checks again," Miro said, tapping on the keys. "Maybe I missed something."

Obi-Wan stared up at the blue screen, trying to read the schematics of the system. Qui-Gon turned away. He knew that Miro was vastly better at figuring out tech systems.

But he could do something that Miro could not. He could go inside the mind of Xanatos.

Qui-Gon closed his eyes, remembering the final scene with Xanatos on the ledge. His enemy's fatal flaw was his need to boast. Often he inadvertently let slip something that would alert Qui-Gon to the diabolical windings of his mind.

And Xanatos prided himself on his elegance. Whatever he had done, it would have a twist.

Qui-Gon remembered the fiendish glee in Xanatos' expression. Yes, there was something personal about what he had done, some final, stinging slap to the Jedi.

What you revere can destroy you. . . .

Qui-Gon's eyes sprang open. "Miro, where is the main power source of the system?" he barked.

"In the power core," Miro answered. He crossed the room and opened a durasteel door marked FUSION FURNACE. "Here."

Qui-Gon hurried through the door. He found himself in a small circular room. A catwalk ran around a deep central core. A ladder led down into it.

"This is the fusion reactor. The power sources

are lined up in a grid," Miro explained. "It goes down about ten stories. I'm running my second checkup on the power sources now, but nothing came up the first time —"

"No," Qui-Gon murmured. "It wouldn't."

He hoisted himself onto the ladder and began to climb down. "Whatever you do, don't reboot the system," he called up to Miro.

It didn't take him long to reach the bottom of the core. Qui-Gon circled around slowly, running his hands along the various compartments and dials. He saw a compartment labeled FUSION FURNACE ACCESS.

Qui-Gon pressed the lever. The door slid open. Nestled inside were the stolen Healing Crystals of Fire.

He tucked the glowing artifacts reverently in his tunic. Immediately, they warmed his skin.

He climbed up the ladder where Miro and Obi-Wan were waiting anxiously. He pulled the crystals out of his tunic. "They were in the fusion furnace," he told Miro.

"They would have served as a massive power source," Miro said, his voice slightly unsteady. He cleared his throat. "They would have started a chain reaction with the burst of energy from the reboot. If I had punched that key —"

"What we revere would have destroyed us," Qui-Gon finished.

CHAPTER 20

The Temple returned to normal faster than anyone thought possible. Systems were up and running, students moved back to their quarters, new food shipments arrived, and classes resumed.

Obi-Wan felt out of step. He did not feel normal again. He still remembered the brush of Bruck's fingers against his. Time and again he stared down at his hand and opened and closed his fist, remembering how he had grabbed air instead of Bruck.

Bruck had tried to kill his friend. Obi-Wan was glad that he had stopped him. But he had been responsible for another person's death, and he could not forget it.

Obi-Wan only had one mission now: to talk to Bant.

She had been checked out at the med unit and pronounced in perfect health. The only thing she would need was rest, so she was given a day off from classes.

Obi-Wan searched for her everywhere. At last he found her at the place he least expected — the waterfall. She sat on a rock overlooking the pool where she'd almost died. Bant always sat as close as possible to the pool, so that the fine spray misted her skin.

"Why are you here?" he asked gently, taking a seat beside her.

"This is one of my favorite spots at the Temple," Bant answered, her silver eyes on the cascading water. "I did not want what happened here to spoil that. I almost died here. Someone else did lose his life. The experience taught me more about being a Jedi than a thousand classes." She turned to Obi-Wan. "I hope you don't blame yourself for Bruck's death."

"I know I tried my best to save him," Obi-Wan said. "But my heart is still heavy."

"That is how it should be," Bant said. "A life is lost. When he still had life, he had a chance to change."

"Bant, I am so sorry for —" Obi-Wan began in a rush.

"Don't," Bant interrupted softly. "There's no need to apologize. You saved my life, you know."

"There is a need," Obi-Wan said firmly. "There is a great need." He stared down at his hands in his lap. "I spoke out of anger and jealousy. What I felt mattered to me more than your feelings."

"You were worried about your future," Bant said. "You are afraid of losing Qui-Gon."

Obi-Wan sighed. He stared out at the sapphire pool. "I thought I could return to the Temple and everything would be as it was. The Council would excuse me and welcome me back. Qui-Gon would come around. But I am the one to come around. I see now that what I did cannot be fixed so easily. It may never be fixed. I see what I've done to myself, to the Master–Padawan relationship. This is why a Jedi waits so long and is so careful about choosing a Padawan. So much trust is involved. I ask myself, if Qui-Gon had rejected me, set me loose after I pledged my life to his, how would I feel? Yes, I would forgive him, but could I join him again? Could I deliver all my trust to him again?" He met Bant's eyes, feeling desolation well inside him. "I don't know the answer," he finished. "How can I expect Qui-Gon to know?"

"I think you could trust him again," Bant said slowly. "And I think Qui-Gon will do the same. All of this just happened. You haven't had time to sit down and think, let alone talk to each other. You've been through so much. There are things that happened on Melida/Daan you won't tell me." She paused delicately. "When you are ready, I would like to hear them."

Obi-Wan took a shuddering breath. He could not say her name aloud. But somehow he knew he must. He knew that if this moment passed, he might never speak of her again to a living soul, and something in him would die.

"Her name was Cerasi," he said. He felt a great tide of sorrow rise in him. But he also felt a release by saying her name. "Cerasi," he said again. He lifted his face and felt the cooling spray. Suddenly, he felt stronger, as though Cerasi's vibrant spirit stood by him and touched his shoulder. "We had a connection that I can't explain. It wasn't the result of time, of hours spent together. It wasn't the result of secrets or confidences. It was something else."

"You loved her," Bant said.

Obi-Wan swallowed. "Yes. She inspired me. We fought together side by side. We trusted each other. And when she died, I blamed myself. When I thought that you might die, I knew I could not go on if it happened."

"But you would have, Obi-Wan," Bant said softly. "We all go on." She leaned against him, her eyes sparkling with unshed tears. "You saved my life. We will go on together."

*   *   *

Qui-Gon sat in Tahl's quarters. They had been silent for some time. TooJay had been sent for reprogramming. For once, Qui-Gon would have welcomed her musical chatter.

"You are to meet the Council soon," Tahl said at last. "If you decide to take Obi-Wan back as your Padawan, it will help him. The Council would most likely allow him to come back."

"I know," Qui-Gon said.

"Especially considering all he has done," Tahl added.

"I am well aware of all he has done."

Tahl sighed. "You are a stubborn man, Qui-Gon."

"No," Qui-Gon protested. "Not stubborn. Cautious. I must be sure, Tahl. What if taking Obi-Wan back is not fair to the boy, or to the Jedi? If I cannot give Obi-Wan my trust, our Master–Padawan bond will eventually break."

"And you feel you cannot rebuild that trust?" Tahl asked.

Qui-Gon looked down at his hands in his lap. "It is my flaw, I know."

Another silence stretched between them. Then Tahl picked up her cup and ran her fingers around the smooth surface. She held it up to the light she could not see.

"This is a beautiful cup," she said. "I know this even though I can't see it. I can feel it."

It was beautiful, Qui-Gon saw. The material was so thin it was almost translucent, the color a blue so pale it was almost white. The shape was simple, with no handle or curved rim.

"I use it even though I may break it," she said. She placed it down carefully. "Have you ever heard of the planet Aurea?"

"Of course," Qui-Gon said. "Aurea is noted for its fine artisans."

"They have the best glass workers in the galaxy there," Tahl went on. "Many have wondered why this world has advanced the art so much. Is it the golden sands, the temperature of the fires, the long tradition? Whatever it may be, they make the most beautiful vessels in the galaxy, so highly prized that they are priceless objects. But occasionally, someone is careless, or an accident occurs, and one is broken."

Tahl picked up her cup again. "Just like I could break this cup. But these artisans have a greater art than the fashioning of the vessels. They remake the shattered ones. And in that remaking they find their highest art. They take the pieces of something beautiful that has been smashed and create something even more beautiful. You see the seams of the break, but the piece is still flawless. Because it had once been broken, it becomes more valuable than before."

Tahl placed the blue cup before Qui-Gon. The

Jedi sat in silence, absorbing the lesson. Could it be, he wondered slowly, that the process of rebuilding his trust with Obi-Wan would not be painful, but satisfying?

He picked up the delicate cup. It almost disappeared in his large hand. His fingers closed around the fragile shape, yet the cup did not break.

He could not make again what he'd had. But what if the new thing he made was stronger than before, because it had once been broken?

CHAPTER 21

Qui-Gon stood before the Jedi Council with Obi-Wan by his side. They had finished their debriefing on the episode with Xanatos.

Obi-Wan noted Qui-Gon's frown with dismay. He sensed the roiling unrest in his former Master.

Obi-Wan himself had reason to feel satisfied. The Council had also delivered news to him. Obi-Wan had humbly asked not to be taken back, but to be given probation. It had been granted. He would be required to remain on Temple grounds and have sessions with various Council members. He had not received what he had wanted, but he had received what he felt was right.

But Qui-Gon had not. The Council had opposed Qui-Gon's wish to pursue Xanatos.

"I do not understand your hesitation," Qui-Gon said. "Xanatos is a powerful enemy of the Jedi."

"Enemy of yours, I think he is," Yoda said, his gray-blue eyes intent on Qui-Gon. "Fruitless, a search may be. Wasted energy, it is. And too much anger I sense in you, Qui-Gon. Xanatos will reappear. Meet him you shall. But seek it you shall not."

"We do not forbid you," Mace Windu said. "But know that if you do, you go without our support."

Qui-Gon did not react. He bowed stiffly and turned on his heel. Obi-Wan followed him from the room.

They stood in the hallway together. Obi-Wan saw that Qui-Gon was struggling to contain his emotions. He knew the Jedi Knight was bitterly disappointed.

"You have told me many times that Yoda always turns out to be right," Obi-Wan tried cautiously. "Even when it doesn't seem so."

"Not this time," Qui-Gon said grimly. "I am going after him, Obi-Wan."

Surprised, Obi-Wan fell silent. He knew how much Qui-Gon respected the wishes of the Council. To oppose them must be a wrenching decision.

Then he pictured Qui-Gon alone, hunting his enemy, and an essential truth pierced him. The picture was wrong. There was a piece missing. Even if Qui-Gon couldn't see it, Obi-Wan could.

Look for

JEDI APPRENTICE
The Day of Reckoning

Qui-Gon was still brooding about the escape of Xanatos, Obi-Wan knew. Anger was not an appropriate emotion for a Jedi, but Obi-Wan sensed Qui-Gon's taut frustration. He had faced Xanatos in battle, and had been forced to let his opponent escape in order to save the Temple.

Obi-Wan knew that moment still haunted Qui-Gon. He had come close to stopping Xanatos. It made him even more determined to bring him to justice now. Qui-Gon felt strongly that Xantos was a grave threat to the galaxy while on the loose.

Obi-Wan knew that Qui-Gon took this mission personally. Xanatos had once been Qui-Gon's Jedi apprentice, just as Obi-Wan had.

And we both betrayed him, Obi-Wan thought.

His offense, he knew, was not even close to what Xanatos had done. The dark side preyed on Xanatos. He lusted after power and wealth. His every decision moved him closer to evil.

Obi-Wan had betrayed Qui-Gon by abandoning him. He had decided to leave the Jedi order in order to stay to help a planet regain peace. He had come to regret the decision. The Council had agreed that he could rejoin the Jedi, but he was now on probation. Obi-Wan could regain what he had, but he could not seem to regain Qui-Gon's trust. Something essential between them had be violated. Now they were just feeling their way along. On this mission, Obi-Wan hoped to show Qui-Gon that they could restore the bond they had started to form.

The Council had not forbidden him to accompany Qui-Gon — they allowed him to go. Still, his decision had not pleased them. They already had a problem with what they saw as his impulsive decision to leave the Jedi. This latest decision hadn't changed their opinion.

Obi-Wan had to admit that he was relieved to be temporarily out from under the Council's scrutiny as well as the Temple itself. In the final battle, a Jedi student had fallen to his death in front of him. Obi-Wan had not been responsible. Why did the death continue to haunt him? When he had taken off from the Temple grounds, a heaviness had seemed to lift from his heart.

Qui-Gon had considered many ways to enter the planet without detection, but finally decided the simplest way was best. They would arrive among a throng, as tourists.

Telos was a rich planet with many natural beauties. It had a thriving tourist trade and business interests with other planets in the galaxy. Transports were always crowded.

The many travelers made it easy for the Jedi to disappear. They wore nondescript brown cloaks over their tunics and kept their lightsabers hidden. Although Qui-Gon was a powerfully built man with nobel features, he was also capable of dimming his presence and folding into a crowd. Obi-Wan followed his example. They were not recognizable as Jedi, and no one paid the slightest attention to them. Obi-Wan settled back into the plush upholstery and watched as a group of Duros walked by, all speaking in Basic.

"This is my third trip," one of them said. "You're going to love Katharsis."

"They won't let outsiders into the final round," the other said. "That's where you can really score."

Obi-Wan wondered what Katharsis was. Some kind of game? He missed the other's reply, for Qui-Gon had looked up from his datapad at last.

"I think the weak link is UniFy," he said. "We'll start there."

Obi-Wan nodded. UniFy was a Telosian company that the Jedi Master Tahl suspect front for Offworld, the huge minir that spanned the galaxy. Xa company. No one knew where the headquarters were.

Qui-Gon's brows came together in a frown as he gazed at Obi-Wan. Obi-Wan had no idea what he was thinking. Was he worrying about the mission ahead, or was he regretting Obi-Wan's presence?

They had lost the mind connection they had once had. There had been fitful starts and shaky periods in their Master–Padawan relationship from the beginning. Still, there had been many times when Obi-Wan knew what Qui-Gon would ask before he asked it. And Qui-Gon often knew exactly what Obi-Wan was feeling without his having to say a word.

Now Obi-Wan felt a void.

He would be able to feel connected to Qui-Gon again, he told himself. It would just take time. Back at the Temple, the last expression of good-bye from his friend Bant had been one simple word: *patience*.

Obi-Wan and Gui-Gon hadn't had time to re- ~~ve~~ anything. They hadn't had time to argue, or ~~Their~~ decisions. The flurry of departure had landing them. There had been information to ~~is~~ to pack, and good-byes to be said. drew closer to the towers of ~~~~y of Telos. It flew into a ~~~~ with the gentlest of bumps. The public address system announced that the arrival procedures were now underway.

They stood and gathered their packs, then joined the stream of passengers heading for the exit.

Qui-Gon leaned in to speak to Obi-Wan softly. "No doubt he will be hard to find," he said. "He knows that I will pursue him. We will have to flush him out."

The announcement system informed them in a pleasant tone that there would be a slight delay in embarking. Identification would be checked by security police on Telos. Everyone would have to be cleared before leaving the ship.

Passengers began to grumble. Why were security procedures suddenly so stringent? This would take time. They were anxious to reach their destinations.

"I hear they're checking for some escaped criminals," someone said near Obi-Wan's elbow. "Bad luck for all of us."

Through the crowd, Obi-Wan glimpsed the security police herding the passengers into orderly lines. Qui-Gon frowned.

"I wanted to slip in unobserved," he said. "If they discover we are Jedi, it could tip off Xanatos. Tahl said he has bribed many officials here."

With a slight movement of his head, Qui-Gon signaled to Obi-Wan. It was time for them to find their own exit.